W9-BKL-778

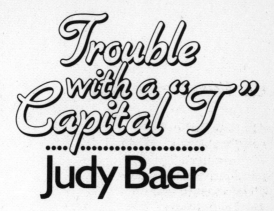

Trouble with a "T"

Judy Baer

BETHANY HOUSE PUBLISHERS
MINNEAPOLIS, MINNESOTA 55438
A Division of Bethany Fellowship, Inc.

Trouble With a Capital "T"
Judy Baer

Library of Congress Catalog Card Number 88–71503

ISBN 1-55661-021-1

Published by Bethany House Publishers
A Division of Bethany Fellowship, Inc.
6820 Auto Club Road, Minneapolis, Minnesota 55438

Printed in the United States of America

Trouble
with a "T"

Cedar River Daydreams

Other Books by Judy Baer

For Nathan Unseth,
who encouraged me,

And for Goldie and Elaine Baron,
who faithfully read my work.

JUDY BAER received a B.A. in English and Education from Concordia College in Moorhead, Minnesota. She has had ten novels published and is a member of the National Romance Writers of America, the Society of Children's Book Writers and the National Federation of Press Women.

Two of her novels have been prizewinning bestsellers in the Bethany House SPRINGFLOWER SERIES (for girls 12–15); *Adrienne* and *Paige*. Both books have been awarded first place for juvenile fiction in the National Federation of Press Women's communications contest.

Chapter One

Lexi Leighton's eyelids fluttered open as sun-beams flooded her room and crept across her pillow. She smiled and stretched until every muscle in her body was humming with energy. After a final, lei-surely stretch and a big, satisfying yawn, she swung her feet to the floor. With her big toe, she searched beneath her bed for her slippers.

It was going to be a great day. She could feel it in her bones. Today was the day she was going to Camp Courage.

"Merrily we row our goat, row our goat; merrily we row our goat, row our goat. . . ." A small, off-key voice floated up the stairs.

It took all of Lexi's willpower not to laugh out loud. She could even *hear* that it was going to be a wonderful day!

"That's *boat*, Ben. Boat! Not goat!" she shouted.

"Merrily we row our boat. . . ."

She grinned as she bent over and pulled a pair of pink satiny slippers from beneath the bed. Lexi ruf-fled her thick golden mane of hair and meandered to the dresser and trifold mirror in the corner of her bedroom. As she stared intently into the mirror, a wide-eyed, pink-cheeked image stared back.

"Alexis, are you awake?" Mrs. Leighton asked as she tapped at the bedroom door. "Ben's been up for two hours waiting for you."

"Sure. Come in, Mom. I just got up."

Mrs. Leighton turned the knob and walked in. Lexi gave her mother a quick glance. Mrs. Leighton was trim, young, and pretty—she could almost be Lexi's older sister—especially in the blue jeans and "Ski North Dakota" sweater she was wearing. Lexi wondered sometimes how she managed to stay so cheerful, considering all the sadness and hurt her mother had suffered over Ben. Having a child with Down's syndrome couldn't have been easy, even with a sweet-natured child like Ben.

"Are you going to be doing any painting today?"

"Inside or out?"

"Either one." Mrs. Leighton had taken up oil painting as a hobby when they'd moved to Cedar River only a few weeks before. She had been walking around with paint under her fingernails ever since.

"I think I'll paint the porch today since you and Ben aren't going to be around. That's four less feet to make prints before it's completely dry."

"That reminds me," Lexi gasped, "I'd better get going. Todd is going to pick us up any minute."

Todd Winston. He'd started out as Ben's "best friend" and now he was Lexi's as well. His mother was the administrator of Camp Courage, a day camp for the handicapped.

"What exactly is it that you and Todd are going to do today?"

"He calls it 'Olympic training' because of all the talk at camp about the Special Olympics. Mrs. Winston says it's his excuse to play with the kids outside of the organized activities at camp. Some of the kids with working parents really enjoy having Todd give them some extra attention." Lexi grinned as she pulled on a pair of red shorts and a white sweatshirt. "I'm not sure who gets more excited, the campers or Todd."

"Well, Ben is certainly excited. He's been dancing around the kitchen singing all morning." Mrs. Leighton smiled. "After his rocky start here in Cedar River, I think Ben has learned to love this place—and Camp Courage is the reason."

Lexi pulled a brush through her curly blond hair and tied it in place with a bright red ribbon as her mother watched.

"There's juice on the table—if Ben hasn't already spilled it."

"Thanks, Mom." Just then Ben bolted through the doorway.

"Go, Lexi! Let's go!" He stood on the threshold, his sturdy legs locked into place and his arms crossed impatiently over his chest. His dark hair glinted in the morning light and his almond-shaped eyes sparkled. "Go now!"

Lexi complied, taking Ben's hand and leading him downstairs to the kitchen. As Lexi poured a bowl of cereal, Mrs. Leighton leaned against the counter, her expression intent.

"It's good to have you back, Lexi," she finally commented.

"Huh?"

"Welcome back, Lexi Leighton!"

"What's that supposed to mean?" Lexi asked, feeling a little silly. Still, she had an idea what her mother meant.

"When we first moved here, I was afraid I'd lost you. You turned from that crazy, fun-loving, independent girl I'd known into a very quiet, lonely stranger."

"It was pretty scary, Mom. Leaving all my friends behind. I was afraid I'd never make any new ones. And," she added more to herself than to her mother, "I sure made some mistakes—like thinking the Hi-Five Club was where I belonged."

"Well, that's over now. You've got Todd and Peggy and Jennifer and I don't know how many others calling you on the phone. Pretty soon you're going to have to pay me to be your answering service."

"Okay, here's payment in full." Lexi leaned over and gave her mother a kiss on the forehead. "Tell anyone who calls today that I'm at Camp Courage. Come on, Ben. I see Todd pulling into the driveway right now."

Ben ran ahead toward Todd's 1949 Ford coupe, while Lexi followed slowly behind. *Friendship.* She had a first-rate one with Todd. Even though she and Minda Hannaford and Jerry Randall had never been able to resolve their differences, she'd learned a lesson from them. Never again would she go against her own conscience to please others. She wouldn't conform just for the sake of being part of a group. She straightened her shoulders and lengthened her stride. Todd was just going to have to like the most determined *non*-conformist in Cedar River!

"Ready?" Todd leaned over and opened the door for Lexi from the inside of the car. As she slid in, the prickly seat cover pulled at the backs of her thighs.

"Sure. But not as ready as Ben."

"Hey, little fellow! Are you ready to play? This big fellow is!"

"Play," Ben echoed from the backseat where he was already engrossed in a puzzle Todd had left out for him.

Todd turned toward Lexi. "It's nice of you to come to help out. Really, all I'm going to do is tell the kids what the rules will be, and run a few practice relays." He grinned sheepishly. "I just like seeing the kids have fun."

When they reached Camp Courage, Todd pulled into the "Reserved" parking spot next to his mother's red Ford hatchback. Lexi squirmed impatiently in her seat. She could hardly wait to get out and look around.

Camp Courage lived up to its name.

"It's beautiful!" Lexi gasped. "I had no idea how pretty it was out here." The camp sat on the edge of a tiny lake, its cabins tucked into the rolling hills and shaded by large old trees.

"Now that you know, will you come back?" Todd smiled proudly as he watched a group of children playing softball from wheelchairs and walkers.

"Definitely. I shouldn't have waited so long."

"Ben, do you want to go to music?" Todd asked.

"Row, row, row your goat. . . ." Ben didn't even look back as he made his way across the field to the gazebo where the children were gathering.

"I didn't realize you had music here too."

"Camp songs mostly. It's one of the kids' favorite activities. It's good for kids like Ben because it gives them a chance to develop socially and participate in a group. They have to follow directions, take turns—that kind of thing. Some of the kids have real trouble communicating, and music is great for language development as well." Todd guided her across the thick carpet of grass as he spoke.

"How'd you get so smart?"

"Probably from living with my mother. This is all she talks about." Todd grinned. "She'd squeeze money out of rocks to get programs for the handicapped—or do handstands down main street if she thought it would help the kids."

"Then that must be where you get your enthusiasm."

"I get it from the kids." Todd's voice softened, and when he spoke again, his voice held an undisguised awe. "These little guys have a million strikes against them, yet *they* keep on going."

She nodded thoughtfully. *Like Ben.*

"Hey, Todd! Are you coming or what?" A lanky, bean-pole of a boy came loping up beside them. "I've got two relay races organized, but you'll have to take one group."

"Egg, I'd like you to meet Lexi Leighton. Lexi, this is Egg McNaughton."

"Egg?"

The boy grinned, revealing a mouth full of metal that sparkled in the sunlight. "My real name is Edward."

"And that's why they call you Egg?"

"No," Todd laughed. "We call him Egg because

McNaughton and McMuffin sound so much alike."

"So they call you Egg McMuf . . . Oh."

Egg grinned and Lexi squinted at the glare. "It's okay. There's a kid at school they call Liver. If you're going to be a protein, I prefer eggs."

"Come on, Lexi. Let's go help Egg with the relay. And there are lots more people I want you to meet."

"Soup and Sandwich, I suppose." The three of them laughed together as they made their way to the race track.

What the Camp Courage kids lacked in coordination and strength, they made up for in determination and enthusiasm—and volume.

"Here, you be the official timekeeper for the races," Todd had instructed. "Egg and I are going to explain the rules to the kids so they won't be surprised or confused when they finally run the races for real."

Nothing went very quickly, Lexi discovered. Even the races. Some of the children had a hard time making it from one end of the track to the other, but she timed each one and cheered equally hard as they crossed the finish line.

"Hi. Are you the official timer?" A small voice came from over her shoulder.

Lexi swung around and almost knocked over the tiny girl behind her. "I'm sorry. I didn't realize you were so close."

"That's okay. I kind of snuck up behind you. It took me a while to get up the courage to say hello."

"It did?" Lexi blinked. "Why?"

"I've heard about you. You're the new girl in town that everyone has been talking about." The girl's eyes grew wise. "It isn't everybody who stands up to the Hi-Five and gets to hang out with Todd Winston."

"Oh. That." Wouldn't people ever forget her near miss with Minda Hannaford and her gang?

The petite girl smiled. "I'm sorry. I didn't introduce myself. I'm Binky McNaughton."

"Binky? As in sister to Egg?"

"Yeah. Terrible, isn't it?"

"Being Egg's sister or being named Binky?"

"Both. I think it's easier to be named Binky, though."

Lexi dropped to the ground beneath a shade tree and curled her legs under her. The races had turned into a free-for-all that didn't warrant a stopwatch. "Want to tell me how you got to be named Binky?"

Binky dropped down beside her. "Sure. My real name is Bonita and I've always been tiny. I'm fifteen, but you'd never know it to look at me."

That was true. Lexi had been wondering if Binky was twelve or thirteen.

"Anyway, my nickname used to be Dinky. Somebody used the *B* from my first name and now I'm Binky." She finished matter-of-factly and then stared at Lexi. "Do you have a nickname?"

"Lexi. That's all."

"That's much nicer than Binky. Lucky you."

"Yeah. But think what a good conversation piece your name is."

"I suppose so. But that's enough talking about me. How do you like Cedar River?"

How *did* she like it here? Lexi turned the question over in her mind. Some parts of it were great— Todd, Camp Courage, Peggy and Jennifer. And some parts were not so great at all. Minda Hannaford and Jerry Randall came immediately to mind.

"So far, so good," Lexi finally murmured. "It's pretty early to tell yet."

Binky nodded wisely. "I didn't like it when we moved here either. But that was because I missed all my friends." She paused. "Now my friends are all here and I like it fine."

Lexi smiled. She liked Binky. This encounter with the tiny girl was a bit like having a humming-bird land next to you and begin to carry on a conversation. Lexi ventured a question.

"Binky, do you know much about Minda Hannaford?"

Binky's expression turned guarded and she paused a moment. "Why?"

"Just asking. Minda and I didn't get off to a very good start when I moved to Cedar River. I've been thinking I should make some kind of an effort to let her know that we could still be friends." It was easy talking to Binky, Lexi decided. It seemed as though they'd known each other a long time—instead of only a few minutes. But, and Lexi smiled to herself, how could anyone *not* like people named Binky and Egg?

"Forgive and forget? Is that what you mean?"

"Sort of. In the Bible it says that we should forgive people for what they do to us. I think it's my responsibility to let Minda know I've done that." Lexi paused. "But it's hard."

"Especially with Minda. She doesn't let anyone get very close." Binky stretched her birdlike legs out in front of her.

"Even Tressa Williams?"

"Tressa? Maybe. But I don't think Minda really confides in anyone." Binky gave Lexi a frank stare. "To tell you the truth, I'd stay away from Minda. She's just trouble. To get close to her you have to play by her rules or not play at all."

"Maybe—"

"Not maybe. For sure. Minda can be nice, but she can also be very cruel."

"Do you know why?"

"Why Minda is mean?" Binky tipped her head. "Probably because she likes to be. She must think it's fun. She's got a rich father and gets everything she wants. I suppose she thinks everyone else should give her what she wants, too."

Lexi nodded slowly. It wasn't a very pretty picture that Binky painted. Somehow, some way, there had to be more good in Minda than Binky believed.

"All I can say is that I wouldn't get on Minda's bad side if I were you," Binky warned. "She can be pretty nasty."

Too late, Lexi thought. She'd been on the wrong side of Minda ever since she moved to Cedar River.

"Do you play tennis?" Binky asked.

"Sure."

"Egg and I are going to play this afternoon. Do you and Todd want to make it doubles?"

"Sounds great, but you'd have to ask Todd."

"Okay. Here he comes with Egg. Hey, guys!"

"What's up?"

"We're playing tennis at two. Want to make it doubles?"

Todd gave Lexi a quick glance.

She nodded.

"We'll be there. And"—Todd jabbed his finger through the air at the pair—"you'll be sorry. We'll cream you."

"Hah!" Egg grinned. "No chance. Two o'clock. School courts."

"You can play tennis, can't you?" Todd whispered.

"And what if I say I can't?"

"I'll be eating tennis balls for an afternoon snack."

"Don't worry. I can hold my own on the tennis court."

Todd gave a wide, satisfied grin.

Later that afternoon, her brave statement came back to haunt her.

I can hold my own on the tennis court.

I meant playing tennis, Lexi thought ruefully. *Not staying cool under the withering stares of Minda Hannaford and her doubles partner, Jerry Randall.*

"Looking good!" Todd had whooped as Lexi came out in her white-and-blue tennis outfit.

"Thanks. Same to you." Todd, tall and bronzed, looked great in his white tennis shorts and pale yellow knit shirt. Lexi wanted to pinch herself. Was she the same girl who had hated Cedar River and found it lonely? Those days seemed long past—until, that is, she and Todd reached the tennis courts.

Egg and Binky were warming up on the closest court, Binky's petite arms and legs seemingly no match for Egg's long, gangly reach. On the next court were Minda and Jerry, both looking as though they'd just stepped out of the pages of a sporting goods advertisement. Tressa Williams and a boy Lexi didn't recognize were playing against them.

After receiving the glare Minda shot her way, Lexi would have felt more welcome in a wasp's nest.

"Don't worry," Todd hissed into her ear. "It's a free country. We have as much right to be here as they do."

Lexi gave him a grateful smile. At least he understood how uncomfortable it was for her to be around someone who disliked her as much as Minda did. Todd and Jerry always seemed to be at odds too.

It was Jerry's fault, Lexi mused. It was as though he was jealous of Todd. That was particularly odd since it was Jerry who had the new, flashy cars, and Todd who drove the old clunkers. If anyone was going to be jealous, it should have been the other way around.

"Let's warm up. I feel a win coming on!" Egg yelled, oblivious to Lexi's discomfort.

"Forget her, Lexi. Forget her," Todd warned.

Forget her? That was pretty difficult, considering what she and Minda had already been through. Minda had asked her to steal in order to become a member of her club, the Hi-Five. And Minda had tried to ruin Lexi's performance in the summer musical by stealing her costume.

Still, what bothered Lexi most of all was that Minda, despite her meanness, seemed almost . . . frightened. Lexi stared hard at the slim blond batting tennis balls at Jerry Randall with a vengeance.

"See?" Todd asked as he came up beside her. "Minda's pretending that you don't exist. You have to do the same."

Todd was right. Minda and Jerry were both acting as though the court to their left was still empty. Lexi picked up a ball and slammed it over the net with as much force as she could muster.

Todd gave a low whistle under his breath. "If you serve them all like that, we'll be forty-five-love in no time."

Lexi grinned. She'd been considered a good player back in her old school. Maybe this was just what she needed—a way to work off steam and build her self-confidence all at once. For the next few minutes, she and the rest of the players forgot everything but the game.

Suddenly, one of Lexi's powerful returns hit Minda square in the back as the girl ran to retrieve a stray ball. Lexi was acutely reminded that friendly forces weren't inhabiting the next court.

"Owww!" Minda stumbled forward, the rubbery toe of her tennis shoe sticking to the asphalt surface. Her arms fanned awkwardly about her body.

"Sorry!" Lexi gasped. "Are you all right?" Out of the corner of her eye, she saw Egg and Binky giggling.

"No thanks to you!" Minda snapped. "You *aimed* for me."

"Of course I didn't!" Lexi protested. "I wouldn't do—"

"Now look what you've done. Your weird friends are laughing at me." Minda sneered in the direction of the McNaughtons. "Of course, they're too stupid to know any better."

"Now, just a minute," Lexi began. "You can't—"

"I can do or say anything I please. Now get away from me." Minda swooshed her hands at Lexi as if she were shooing away a pesky animal. "Get away!"

A blush of humiliation washed across Lexi's cheeks. "I *said* I was sorry."

Minda flipped her head in a defiant gesture.

"And you can't talk that way about my friends," Lexi warned.

Minda threw her a cold blue stare as she commented icily, "I wish you'd been as loyal when you were a Hi-Five member. *Then* you would have had something to be loyal to." She looked witheringly to the far end of the court. "Something better than those two."

Lexi's temper was quickly reaching the boiling point. One part of her wanted desperately to punch the nasty smirk off Minda's face; yet something held her back.

"Back off, Minda," Todd murmured.

"Stay out of it, Winston. Can't your little friend stand up for herself?" Minda challenged.

"What's going on?" Jerry swaggered up to the threesome, tapping his racquet on his knee. His lip turned upward in a half sneer.

Jerry always appears to be looking down on people, acting as if they aren't good enough for him, Lexi thought. *Maybe it is his car or the way he dresses that makes him think he is better than everyone else.*

"Clumsy here nearly knocked me over," Minda said with a scathing look at Lexi. "People who don't know how to play shouldn't be allowed on the courts."

Jerry's amused gaze traveled over the three angry faces. "My, my," he mimicked, "aren't we upset?" Then he asked the question that struck home to Lexi. "Are you sure it's tennis you're fighting over—or something else?"

Minda was about to retort when Lexi offered softly, "I'm sorry I hit you, Minda. I didn't mean to. You'll have to believe that." Then she turned on the heel of her shoe and walked to where Binky and Egg were waiting.

The crunch of rubber or asphalt told her that Todd was directly behind her, but she didn't stop until she was close to the gaping brother and sister.

"What was *that* all about?" Egg yelped.

"You'd think she'd had an injury that required stitches or brain surgery or something for all that fuss," Todd added.

Lexi smiled weakly and glanced at Todd. "I don't know. What do *you* think it was all about?"

"Don't try to figure Minda out," he shrugged. "No one can. Just accept her the way she is. For some reason she's got it in for you, that's all."

Lexi shuddered. "I don't think I've ever come so close to popping someone in the mouth as I did just now. If it hadn't been for what my dad read last night—"

"What was that?" Binky asked quickly, her eyes wide. It was obvious that there was usually not this much excitement in *her* life.

"In our family devotions we're studying the book of Matthew. We're in chapter five, where it says that if anyone hits you on one cheek—"

"You slug him back!" Egg interjected.

"No. You offer to let him hit the other cheek, too."

"Huh?"

"And if someone steals your coat, you should give him the rest of your clothes, too," Todd added.

"Weird," Binky observed.

"And that's not the hardest part," Lexi sighed. " 'Love your enemies and pray for those who persecute you.' "

"Sounds like it was written with Minda in mind," Egg commented. "We don't talk much about the Bible at our house."

"And apparently they don't at the Hannafords' either," Binky concluded.

Lexi smiled. Her anger had ebbed away.

"I would have said something rotten before I got around to thinking," Binky admitted.

"I almost did. Then Jerry said something that helped—"

"Jerry *helped* you? That's a new one. He's the one who's always worried about himself."

"I doubt he meant to. He just asked if we were fighting over tennis—or something else."

"What did he mean by that?"

"I don't know, but I want to find out. Minda hates me. I know she's angry because I dropped out of Hi-Five, but I think there's more to it than that. I'd like to know what it *is* that we're fighting about!"

"I look like a beet," Binky observed, blithely changing the subject. "I wish I could look like that when I'm all hot and sweaty."

"Like a beet?" Lexi mopped at her forehead with the hem of her blouse.

"No. Gorgeous—like you. When I play tennis, my hair sticks to my forehead in little spikes and my cheeks get all blotchy. You look all warm and glowing—like a model or something."

Lexi laughed. "Thanks. I don't believe a word of it, but I needed to hear that anyway."

"Don't let Minda get to you," Binky advised. "She's just jealous."

"Of me?" she asked in surprise.

"You're cute. Todd likes you. You've moved the center of attention away from her. Why shouldn't Minda hate you?"

It still didn't make sense, Lexi mused. She and Minda could be good friends. She'd hoped for that once—but Minda seemed determined never to let it happen.

On their way home from the tennis court, Todd slowed his pace until Lexi was forced to match his step. "Aren't you coming? Does your foot hurt?" he asked.

"No. I'm just thinking."

"About what?"

"Minda."

"Oh."

Lexi swung her racquet at a bush. "I can't get away from her today, can I?"

"Yes and no. Maybe Minda is one person you're just going to have to avoid, Lexi. You got on her bad side and I think you're stuck there."

"Hasn't she heard of forgiving and forgetting?"

"I doubt it. Anyway, I wouldn't stir her up. That's a little like poking a stick into a hornet's nest."

Lexi nodded. Todd was perhaps right. Why look for trouble? Sooner or later trouble would probably find her.

Chapter Two

"I'd like to speak to Alexis Leighton, please. Is this she?"

The voice on the other end of the line was dignified and very businesslike. Lexi glanced at the receiver in surprise, as if the instrument in her hand could give her an explanation about the crisp voice.

"This is Lexi Leighton. May I help you?"

"Alexis, Mrs. Renee Winston here. Todd's mother."

"Mrs. Winston! Hello." Mrs. Winston was a highly respected person in Cedar River. Her picture seemed to appear somewhere in the *River Times* nearly every week. Todd said that when anyone wanted expertise on grant writing, they went to his mother.

What could she want with me? Lexi wondered.

"I understand that you visited Camp Courage the other day."

"Yes." Was there something wrong with that? she wondered. Surely Todd would have warned her if she wasn't supposed to be there.

"And did you enjoy it?"

"Very much. I can understand now why my brother is so eager to go there every day." She couldn't keep the enthusiasm from her voice. "Ben can hardly eat breakfast anymore. He thinks he's going to miss something at camp if he's a second late."

"Good. I'm glad to hear that. Your brother is a very sweet child."

Surely Mrs. Winston had another reason for calling besides inquiring about Ben's attitude toward camp!

"Have you enjoyed your move to Cedar River?" Mrs. Winston asked.

"I guess so. It was hard to leave my friends, but I'm making new ones." Then Mrs. Winston dropped the bombshell.

"According to Todd, you still have some free time in your schedule."

Free time? Too much of it, Lexi thought to herself.

"You could say that. I was a pool lifeguard before we moved and—"

"Actually, that's what I'm calling about. One of the cook's helpers at the camp sprained her ankle and we're short one person in the kitchen. I've been at a loss as to where to find someone to fill in until school starts, and then Todd suggested you . . ." Mrs. Winston's voice trailed away. "Is there *any* possibility that you'd like a part-time job for a few weeks?"

Would she? If Todd's mother had been standing in the room, Lexi would have given her the biggest, tightest hug she could manage—even if Mrs. Winston was wearing one of her unending supply of navy business suits and starched white blouses!

"I'd love to, Mrs. Winston." She could spend every day near Todd and Ben.

"I know that the kitchen isn't the most appealing place to work, unless you *enjoy* peeling potatoes," Mrs. Winston apologized. "But if the kitchen girl comes back early, I'm sure we could find a spot for you during the organized play periods until school begins."

"It's great. When do I start?"

Mrs. Winston chuckled. "I must say, you're the most eager recruit I've ever had."

Lexi laughed. "I've been wondering what to do with myself now that Mrs. Waverly's summer musical is over. A part-time job is the perfect answer."

"Good. Then report to the camp kitchen tomorrow morning about nine. You'll have to stay through lunch cleanup, which means you should be free about two o'clock. The chief cook will tell you what's expected of you."

"Thanks again," Lexi began.

"No, thank *you*. You're helping me out in a pinch, Lexi. I'll remember that. Goodbye."

With a smile that nearly cracked her face in two, Lexi settled the phone into its cradle. A job at Camp Courage! Things were definitely looking up.

But, as always, when life was moving too smoothly in Cedar River, Minda Hannaford stepped onto the scene.

"Peggy? This is Lexi. Want to go out to the mall? I need some new jeans." She paused for effect. "For my new *job*."

"Job! You've got a job? Tell me everything."

Lexi grinned at the receiver. "It's not much, really. Just part-time kitchen help at Camp Courage, but Mrs. Winston says that I can work my way into other things."

"Lucky! I'd give anything to have a job," Peggy moaned. "If my parents didn't travel so much, I could apply for something. As it is, they keep dragging me off to places like New York and Florida and—"

"Poor baby," Lexi laughed. "You do have it rough. Especially when you could be staying home in Cedar River peeling potatoes like I'm going to."

"You know what I mean. And a lot of really neat people work at Camp Courage."

"So are you going to help me buy jeans or not?" Lexi demanded.

"Are you asking me if I can shop and spend *your* money? Of course. I'll be over in ten minutes."

"Make it five."

"Seven."

"Gotcha."

Within twenty minutes, they were parking the Leightons' family car in the parking lot of Cedar River Mall.

"Yum. Stores. I just *love* to shop. Don't you?" Peggy eyed the vast expanse of shops with undisguised glee.

"It's all right, I suppose."

"All right?" Peggy stared at her friend in disbelief. Then her expression softened. "Of course, if I could design and sew clothes like you do, I probably wouldn't be so crazy to shop either. You're as good as a professional."

"Thanks. I know I'm not ready yet, but someday I'd really like to design fashions for a boutique. If they'd have me."

"They'd be crazy not to!" Peggy announced loyally. "Anyway, if dress designing doesn't work out, you can always design houses!"

Lexi smiled at her friend's enthusiasm. It was fun to wander through the stores and look at the designs and then go home to her sketchbook and create her own versions. Still, it was just a hobby. Someday what she really wanted to do was become an architect. Drawing clothing was one thing, but drawing homes and offices ... It excited her just to think about it.

"Here are the jeans," Peggy announced as she dove behind a rack. "Acid washed, stone washed—washed-washed."

"Nothing too faded. If I wear them every day for a month, we can call them mother-washed."

"Bad joke, Leighton."

Lexi grinned and joined her friend in sorting through the rack of clothing.

Nearly two hours had passed when Peggy announced, "I'm getting hungry. How about you?"

"Ravenous. Want to get a hot dog?"

"A hot dog? Today?"

"What's wrong with that? Are you in the mood for a burger? Nachos? A yogurt sundae?"

"No! No! No! We can't eat that stuff *today*. Today is special. You've found your first job in Cedar River. We've got to celebrate!"

"So I'll buy a cherry malt to go with my hot dog."

"This will be my treat. We're going to eat at The Station."

"You're kidding, right?" Lexi gasped.

The Station was one of the most elite restaurants in town. It had been decorated to resemble the gracious dining cars of turn-of-the-century trains. The tablecloths and napkins were of crisp white linen and the cutlery was sterling silver. Even the sugar came in tiny wrapped cubes instead of mashed into a cup with packets of artificial sweetener. The waiters wore burgundy jackets with bright gold buttons and carried a linen towel over one arm when they served.

"No. This is a day of monumental importance." Peggy looked very important herself as she made that announcement. "Anyway, the lunches aren't too expensive if you order the special. Maybe today it's hot dogs. What do you say?"

"Why not? Once I start working, I won't be free for lunch anymore. I think we owe it to ourselves."

"Good." Peggy beamed. "I wonder if they have escargot . . ."

Lexi caught up with her friend as they hurried down the side corridor on which The Station was located. "If you're going to order snails, I'm getting frogs legs."

Peggy skidded to a halt in front of the elaborately framed menu in the window of The Station and studied the prices. "Sorry to disappoint you, but my baby-sitting money isn't going to pay for either one." Just then a tall, thin woman in jet black drifted toward them.

"Luncheon for two?"

They nodded mutely.

"Follow me, please." She led them through the large main dining room into a small side room. The artificial windows lining the walls had scenes of pastures and grazing cattle.

"We must be traveling through the country now," Peggy hissed.

"Keep your voice down," Lexi whispered.

They entered still another room, this one lined with high-backed booths and flickering candlelight. The ghostly specter of a hostess ushered them into the booth with a flick of her hand. Peggy settled back and opened the massive menu.

"The special today is knockwurst on a sesame-seed bun with a side of cole slaw or potato skins."

Lexi and Peggy stared at each other and willed themselves not to giggle. Finally Lexi inquired, "Is that anything like a hot dog?"

The woman gave her a cold glare and a brief nod and turned away.

"I told you so! I knew they'd have hot dogs here!" Peggy giggled.

Lexi was too busy studying her surroundings to respond. She was cocooned in dark walnut and red velvet inside the booth. The voices of the other patrons were whispering around them, muted by the thick fabrics of the room. Only the voices in the booth directly behind Lexi could be heard clearly. And no matter how hard she tried to ignore them, they carried directly into Lexi's unwilling ear.

"You don't have to be so difficult about this. It's not the end of the world."

"How do you know? Maybe it is for me!"

"Don't be so dramatic. You should be on stage the

way you carry on sometimes."

"It's not funny, Mother! Not funny at all. If Daddy—"

"I don't want to talk about your father. Not now and certainly not with you. The man is a beast, pure and simple. Eat your lunch."

"I'm not hungry."

"Pout then. Behave like a baby. Honestly, I thought I'd get some support from you about this."

"You want me to tell you it's all right for you and Dad to separate? Is that what you expected me to say?"

"Hardly, but I thought the least you could do is try to understand. You know your father's temper. I—"

"But he's my father!"

The voices were escalating. Lexi willed herself not to listen. This argument between the faceless mother and daughter was none of her business.

Peggy gave her a worried look. She, too, could hear the rising voices on the other side of the divider.

"Waitress! Waitress! Another drink, please. Make that a double."

"Mother!"

"Don't nag at me. I need this—"

A clatter of glassware punctuated the sentence. Lexi could feel the occupant of the other side of her booth sliding out.

"You make me sick!"

The sound of shattering crystal made Peggy's eyes grow round and wide with alarm. Lexi took a sip of water to ease the dryness in her mouth. If she ever wanted to be somewhere else, it was now.

"I can't reason with you until you calm down. I—"

A jean-clad figure swept by their booth.

"Minda!" Peggy gasped.

Minda stopped to stare at the pair in the booth, her teary gaze traveling from Lexi to Peggy and back again. When Minda spoke, her voice was harsh. "You? How dare you?"

Peggy and Lexi exchanged a confused look.

"You were spying on me!" Then the weak veneer of bravado crumbled and her tears came. "I hate you! I hate all of you . . ." and she was gone.

Mrs. Hannaford appeared around the corner of the booth, squinting against the weak light over their table. "Who's back here . . . Oh, hello." Her words were oddly slurred. "Don't pay any attention to us, girls. A little family disagreement, that's all."

With that, Mrs. Hannaford made her unsteady way toward the front of the restaurant.

"I think I'm going to die." Peggy lifted a napkin to her lips and looked as though she wanted to be sick. "What are we going to do?"

"I don't know." Lexi heard the quiver in her own voice and felt a wave of nausea overtake her.

"I never realized Minda's mother was like *that*! No wonder Minda is so . . . so . . ."

"Unhappy?"

"I guess that's it. I always figured it was just plain meanness with Minda. I mean, I never knew she had a reason for acting so rotten."

"No one ever has a good reason for that," Lexi murmured softly, her eyes still on the doorway through which Minda and Mrs. Hannaford had left.

"So what do you think we should do? Talk to

Minda? Pretend we didn't hear their fight?"

"I wish we *hadn't* heard the fight, but we did. It won't do any good to tell people about this. It will only embarrass Minda more."

The girls finished their lunch in silence, the celebration forgotten. All the way home, Lexi turned the situation over in her mind. Mrs. Leighton was on the porch as she returned home.

"My, don't you look grim. No jeans? No sales?"

"I wish that was it." And she related the battle scene that had taken place at The Station.

"Minda's made it hard for me from the start, but I'd never wish the fight we heard onto anyone. I'd like to help her, but I think my overhearing the argument has made things even worse. She hates me more than ever now."

"There's always one thing you can do," Mrs. Leighton remarked softly. "It can't hurt."

Lexi nodded and an overpowering sense of relief overtook her. At least she could turn Minda and her problems over to God's protective care.

Chapter Three

"If I see one more potato I'm going to throw up."

"Good day at work?" Todd inquired with a smile. "I loved the fries at lunch."

"Yuk!"

"How many pounds of potatoes did you say you peeled?"

"Don't ask." Lexi stared at her red, chapped hands. They were so nicked and scarred from the dull potato peeler she'd inherited from the last kitchen girl that she looked as though she'd done battle with a meat grinder—and lost.

"Somehow I thought it would be more glamorous than this. Peel potatoes, wash dishes, peel potatoes, wash dishes."

"That was your 'breaking in' period. New people always get the scuzziest jobs. Just wait, it gets better."

"Peel carrots, wash floors, peel—"

"Maybe not *that* good!"

Lexi groaned. "Remind me why I wanted to work here. I've forgotten."

"To be near me?"

Lexi laughed out loud. "That's it! Now I feel better."

Todd grinned. He took her elbow and steered her toward the '49 coupe. "Need a ride?"

"It would be nice. I rode with Dad and Ben this morning, but I'm on foot now."

"Hop in. I promised my brother I'd help him out at the garage at three, so I don't have much time." A worried frown flickered across his features. "I'd better get there on time or he's going to fire me."

Lexi gaped at him openmouthed. "Your brother would *fire* you for being late? Is he *that* tough to work for?"

Todd settled himself against the driver's seat, draped his right arm over the steering wheel, and stared out at the green rolling hills of Camp Courage. "No. Mike's not hard to work for at all—usually."

"So what's going on now?" Lexi didn't like the troubled look that haunted Todd's eyes.

"I'm not sure."

"Huh?"

Todd's mouth twisted into a weak, unhappy smile. "There's been some trouble at the garage, that's all."

"What kind of trouble?"

"Things disappearing. Tools."

"But what does that have to do with you?" Lexi wondered. "You wouldn't take anything from your brother."

"No, but the things that have disappeared were things I'm responsible for." Seeing the blank look on Lexi's face, Todd hurried to explain. "My brother has a system for his mechanics. When a mechanic comes to work for Mike, he usually has his own set of tools. They're very expensive and a lot of guys like working with their own equipment. If a fellow *doesn't* have his own tools, Mike will check out a set to him. That means the guy is responsible for that set and has to make sure it stays together."

"But why wouldn't they stay together? You're talking as if they have little legs or something!"

Todd chuckled. "That's one way of putting it. Mine seem to have developed them, anyway. I've lost several pieces out of my kit lately and I have no idea where they are."

"How's that possible?" Lexi asked.

"It's not so hard to imagine." Todd gave a frustrated shrug. "Sometimes when a guy is done working on an engine, he might just lay a wrench somewhere on top of the motor and accidentally forget it. He closes the hood and the wrench drives off when the owner comes to pick up the car." He grinned. "Once I saw a whole mitt full of tools ride out of the garage on the back bumper of a Chevrolet."

"But wouldn't someone find the tools and return them?"

"That's what Mike is hoping. Every set of tools that's checked out has a different marking. We're both hoping that whoever found them will call. Otherwise, I'm going to have to pay for them."

"Is that expensive?" Lexi wondered.

"Let's just say I'll be working the entire summer for my brother for no wages."

"Ouch."

"Yeah," Todd sighed, and scraped his fingers through his golden hair.

"That's terrible!"

He gave her a melting smile. "Don't worry about it, Lexi. I'm hoping that everything shows up soon." He shook his head. "It's just that I'm usually so *careful* . . ." He shrugged. "But let's talk about something else . . . like school." His expression brightened. "Just wait until school starts, Lexi. You're going to love Cedar River High."

She hoped so. But moving from a school of two hundred to one that was more than triple that size was pretty intimidating. She'd never been shy or timid, but then again, she'd never made a move quite this big before either.

"What's it like, Todd?"

"Action packed. Most of the teachers aren't too bad. Mr. Derek, the coach, is a great guy. So's Mrs. Drummond; she's our class adviser. Cedar River's basketball team has been undefeated for three seasons."

"Thanks to anybody I know?"

"Maybe." He grinned. "Egg McNaughton is our student manager. He keeps us in line."

"The school has a terrific music department. The Emerald Tones is the choir to try out for."

"What's that?"

"It's like a swing choir. We have our own costumes and we can do any music we like. The Emeralds usually get to do a tour in the spring."

Lexi filed the information in the back of her head for future reference.

"Of course, there are several clubs. The usual school-organized ones like Science Club, Computer Club, the Journalism Club . . ."

"And a few that the school *hasn't* organized?"

He shot her a glance. "Yeah."

"Like the Hi-Five?"

"That's one of them."

"I don't think I need any more information on Cedar River's social clubs. I've had enough of them to last a lifetime!"

"Just remember, Minda Hannaford doesn't belong to all of them."

Lexi was relieved that Todd was pulling into the driveway of her home. The last person she wanted to talk about right now was Minda.

She hadn't had the time or opportunity to see Minda since she had overheard the fight at The Station, but Lexi suspected that Minda wasn't too eager to see her, either. Lexi had a hunch that her knowledge of Minda's and her mother's behavior would be hard on the kind of image Minda wanted so hard to project.

Lexi sat on the porch swing and watched Todd drive away. She chewed thoughtfully on her upper lip and set the swing to rocking in its back-and-forth drifting motion. One thing Lexi prided herself on was her ability to read people—their feelings, their attitudes, sometimes even their aspirations. And what she was reading in Minda spelled trouble with a capital T.

Lexi had just gone to her bedroom and curled up to take a quick nap when she heard Jennifer's and Peggy's voices in the living room.

"Lexi, are you here? Lexi?"

"Up here. In the bedroom."

Jennifer and Peggy trooped up the stairs and

flung open the door. "Lying down?"

"In the summer?"

"Give me five minutes, you guys. I'm whipped."
Lexi snuggled deeper into the bedspread.

"I suppose we should let her rest," Jennifer said.
"So she's in shape for the party."

"Yeah. From the sound of it, it's going to be a
great one."

"So just sleep, Lexi. Save your strength."

Lexi propped herself up on her elbows and stared
at the pair standing in her doorway. "Party? What
party?"

It was as though she'd waved a wand and erased
their smiles. Peggy's eyes grew wide. "You haven't
heard about Minda's party?"

Minda. Lexi groaned and dropped back onto the
bed. "No. Was I supposed to?"

"I thought everyone in town got an invitation,"
Jennifer murmured. "She even invited me—and she
was furious at me for dropping out of Hi-Five."

"And me," Peggy added. "I heard as much of that
. . . you know . . . as you did." Lexi and Peggy had
agreed not to breathe a word to anyone of the fight
between Minda and her mother.

Lexi flopped from her back to her stomach. "When
did these invitations come?"

"Yesterday. At least that's when Jennifer's and
mine came."

"And Binky said there was one for her and Egg
too."

"Minda invited Egg *and* Binky?" That was surprising. Minda had never acted as though either of
them existed before now.

"Maybe you should check your mailbox. You probably just haven't gotten yours yet," Jennifer offered hopefully.

Lexi scooted to the side of the bed and swung her feet to the floor. "Good try, Jen, but I got the mail both yesterday and today. There isn't going to be any invitation for me."

"But *everybody* is going to be there!" Peggy wailed.

"Not everybody," Lexi murmured softly. Then she smiled, pretending a happy expression she didn't feel for the sake of her friends. It wouldn't help to let them know how hurt she felt. Even if she and Minda didn't get along, it was hard to be the only one of your friends not invited.

"Don't look so glum, you guys!" she chided. "I probably wouldn't have gone to Minda's party even if I had been invited! There's no use going somewhere you aren't wanted."

She wished her friends would leave. It was so difficult acting nonchalant when all she really wanted to do was yell and pound at her pillow and wonder out loud what it was she'd done to make Minda hate her so.

"You're so brave, Lexi," Peggy murmured. "I'd be crying right now if I were you."

Lexi shrugged. "It's okay, guys. Really. But I'd like to finish my nap now. I got pretty tired at work today."

Jennifer poked Peggy with her elbow. "Come on. We can come back later." She looked hopefully at Lexi. "Call us?"

"Sure. When I get up." Lexi sank back against

the satiny pillow shams and closed her eyes. When she heard footsteps descending the stairs and the front door close, she opened her eyes again.

Minda strikes again.

Lexi stared at the ceiling, her eyes fixed on the white and yellow light fixture of daisies and stems and leaves all wrapped into a circle around the bulb. When she closed her eyes, a single tear trickled from beneath her lid. It lay poised there for a moment at the crest of her cheek before she sat bolt upright and whisked it away.

Minda couldn't do this to her. Minda couldn't make her cry. She could only do it to herself—she could allow herself to cry over Minda's inexplicable resentment toward her. She reached for the Bible on her nightstand. Surely it must say something about times like this. It had held words of comfort and wisdom for every other event in her life.

The pages fell open to Luke. Lexi skimmed the passages until her gaze snagged on the familiar words that now seemed to jump off the page with neon brightness.

"Love your enemies, do good to those who hate you, bless those who curse you, pray for those who abuse you. To him who strikes you on the cheek, offer the other also; and from him who takes away your cloak do not withhold your coat as well. . . . And as you wish that men would do to you, do so to them."

"Oh, great," Lexi murmured. This wasn't what she'd been hoping for at all. Loving Minda? Doing good deeds for her? Praying for her? Treating Minda just like Lexi would want Minda to treat her? Lexi sighed. God hadn't made it easy this time. Not easy at all.

Still, she didn't want go to a party where she wasn't welcome. Lexi had to remind herself of that fact a dozen times over the next few days—every time someone else asked her if she was going to the party.

"It sounds like everyone is going to be there," Egg marveled. "Even me."

"Even you? Hey, Egg, give yourself some credit!" Todd was lying flat on his back on the Leighton porch with his feet propped in the seat of a lawn chair. He rolled his head to the right and glanced at Binky and Lexi who were setting up a puzzle on a card table at the end of the porch. "Right, ladies?"

"Doesn't he know?" Binky whispered.

Lexi shook her head. "Not yet. I guess he just assumes I've been invited."

"*Right*, ladies?" Todd demanded. Taking a look at the expression on their faces, he swung his legs off the chair and rolled to his feet in an easy, fluid motion. "What's going on here?"

Binky, never one for keeping things to herself, blurted, "Lexi didn't get an invitation to the party."

"But everyone—"

"Not quite everyone." Lexi gave a weak smile. "That would be too much to expect of Minda, don't you think? After all we've been through."

"But she's always just issued a blanket invitation to these parties before. I never thought—"

"It's okay. Don't worry about it," Lexi grinned. "In fact, I've got *plans*."

"Plans? Without me?" Todd had become a familiar fixture around the Leighton household as had Peggy, Jennifer and the McNaughtons.

"You didn't tell me that," Binky murmured. "What plans?"

"I've got a date."

Even Egg sat up a little straighter in his chair. "Really? Who?"

"I'm not sure I should tell you."

"Give us a hint," Binky begged. "Just a little one."

Todd was unusually quiet.

"He's tall. Six two. And he has dark brown hair."

"A basketball player, maybe? They're tall." Binky absorbed herself in the puzzle.

"Nice eyes. Kind of greenish, brownish, grayish. Hazel colored."

"Who looks at the color of a guy's eyes," Egg snorted. "Give us another hint."

"He plays racquetball and squash, he jogs five miles a day, and he collects coins."

"I don't know any guys who do that," Binky said. "Is he from Cedar River?"

Lexi was enjoying this. Egg and Binky were both scratching their heads in puzzlement. Then she noticed Todd. His eyes were dark, as though a storm had blown in over a clear blue pond, and tense lines were etched at the corners of his mouth.

Suddenly the game didn't seem quite so funny.

"And he drives a Thunderbird."

The storm clouds scattered. "Your dad drives a Thunderbird," Todd accused.

"You're going out on a date with your *father*?"

"You bet."

"Ohhhhh," Egg groaned and slouched back into his seat. "Is that all?"

" 'Fess up, Leighton. What's going on?"

"Yeah, Lexi, what's going on?"

"I just thought if everyone else in Cedar River was going out, I should too. So I asked my dad for a date. We're going to The Station for escargot, rack of lamb and cherries jubilee."

"Just you and your dad?"

"Yup." It was difficult to keep from laughing, Lexi thought, watching the expressions on the faces of her friends.

"What about your mom and Ben?"

"Macaroni and cheese at the kitchen table."

"You're joking!"

"Would you take *your* mother and little brother on a date?"

"No, but—"

"Well, then?"

Egg groaned and unfolded himself to a standing position. "Come on, Binky. I've got to get you out of here before you get any crazy ideas."

"You're too much, Lexi!" Binky stared at her with admiration. "I would be feeling so sorry for myself if I weren't invited and you—"

"Come *on*, Bink! Let's go."

Binky gave Egg an irritated glance, but she hurried away after her brother.

Todd remained quiet. Finally, when he spoke, his words were soft. "You gave me a scare, Lexi."

"I did?"

"Yeah. For a minute I thought someone was moving in on my territory."

"Your territory?" The idea was flattering. "I can't go steady, Todd. My parents won't allow it. They only approve of group activities."

"I know that. I just wondered for a minute if there was someone new in the group. I could even handle that—as long as I didn't get pushed out."

Lexi moved across the porch until she was standing very close to Todd. She reached out and laid a hand on his arm. "No matter what, I'll never have another friend quite like you." She hurried on before the words stuck in her throat. "You've been so nice to me ever since we moved to Cedar River that I don't know what I would have done without you."

A faint blush stained his features. Then Todd shook his head. "You've been acting so 'up' that it never even occurred to me that Minda had pulled another one of her dirty tricks and left you off the invitation list." His expression grew grim. "I hate to say it, but I think she's invited us—Egg, Binky, and the rest—just to make sure you feel left out. I know for a fact that Egg and Minda *do not* get along. She always makes fun of him—no matter who's around."

"And he's got a secret crush on her, right?"

"So you figured that one out?"

"I'd have to be blind not to." It didn't take much of her skill at reading people to see the longing looks Egg cast at Minda—or the wounded expressions he wore when she sent another barb his way.

"But that's beside the point. We're talking about you now."

"I'm fine, Todd. Really. Have fun at the party and tell me all about it."

"I won't go. We can get a pizza and—"

"Hey! I have a date, remember?"

"Yeah, but—"

"No 'buts' about it. Dad and I are going to have a

terrific time. Don't feel sorry for me." Her expression grew thoughtful. "It hurts to be left out. Especially when you have a hunch that the entire party was designed to make you feel rejected, but I refuse to let Minda decide how I'm going to feel."

Lexi straightened her shoulders. "For a while after I moved to Cedar River, I forgot who was in charge of my life. I let other people push me around. Now I've got it straight again. *I'm* in charge of my life— and God's in charge of me. We're a good team."

"Are you sure?"

Lexi smiled at the pained expression on Todd's face. "Positive. The only way Minda can hurt me is if I let her. I can't control what she does, but I can control how I feel about the things that happen. And I've decided to feel good—my dad and I are going to have a *great* time."

"You're too much." He paused. "I'd really like to stay home and—"

"No way. You guys take notes." Lexi gave a weak smile. "I want to hear all the details about the big bash of the summer. It's going to be fine—really."

Todd chucked her under the chin with his fist. "Attagirl, Leighton."

He turned to lope down the porch steps and across the yard. With a wave he disappeared into the '49 coupe, and in a moment the car disappeared around the corner.

"Right. 'Attagirl, Leighton,' " Lexi mumbled as she turned to go inside. She wasn't going to let Minda get to her. No how, no way. But it was also going to be murder knowing where all her friends were going on Saturday night.

Chapter Four

Saturday dawned clear and beautiful.

It goes to show, Lexi thought to herself, how deceiving looks can be. The brave front she'd put on for Todd and the McNaughtons was still in place, but shaky at the edges. She would be glad when this much-talked-about party was over and she and her friends could get back to normal.

Binky had worried about having the right dress until Lexi finally offered to loan her the sundress she'd been saving for a special occasion.

Lexi glanced out the window to see her friend turning into the front gate. She gathered up the sundress in its plastic suit bag and carried it to the front door.

"Here it is, ready to go." She pushed the dress toward Binky, hoping to avoid another round of thank you's.

"This is really too much, Lexi. I've never had a friend who was willing to do this for me. I—"

"Wear and enjoy. That's all I ask."

"About that—"

"About wearing? Or enjoying?"

Binky pushed her way into the house, past Lexi and into the living room. There, she threw herself against the couch with a force surprising in one so tiny.

"I'm not going."

"Of course you are. I took up the hem and everything. You'll look wonderful. 'A Midsummer Night's Dream.' That will be you. You'll look like a dream."

"I'm not going. If you aren't, I won't. It's just not fair. Minda's being mean and I don't like it. Egg's going to stay home too. We're staging a protest."

"Oh no, you aren't." Lexi dropped the dress onto the boot bench in the hallway and followed her friend into the living room. "I won't let you."

"We want to. Anyway," Binky added wistfully, "Minda just invited us to make you even madder. She's never invited us to a party before."

Lexi felt a tug in her chest. The McNaughtons weren't in the same financial class as the Hannafords. And yet, as much as Binky longed to go to the Hannafords' big house for a party, she'd give it up to remain loyal to a friend.

"I want you to go."

"We can't!" Binky wailed. "We can't leave you behind!"

"Listen to me. Thank you for offering. It's like I told Todd, I never dreamed that God would give me such wonderful friends in Cedar River. Todd has offered to stay home with me and so have Jennifer and Peggy. And I told every one of them the same thing I'm telling you. Go! Have fun. Please?"

"You mean it? Really and truly mean it?"

"You think I'd lie?"

"No."

"Well, then?"

"And you and your father are going to have dinner at The Station?"

"The works." Lexi pulled Binky to her feet. "Now get out of here. You have to do your hair."

Still looking unsure, Binky disappeared down the sidewalk, toting the dress bag.

Just then, Mrs. Leighton walked into the hallway and put her hands on her daughter's shoulders.

"Will you forgive your mother for doing something foolish?" Mrs. Leighton asked.

"Sure. Did you fix chicken croquettes for lunch again?"

"Worse than that, I'm afraid."

Lexi spun around on tiptoe. "Sounds serious."

"Elenore Pierce just called from the Hospital Auxiliary. They're sponsoring a bazaar in the park tomorrow afternoon to raise money for charity. Our church is having a table of baked goods."

"So?"

"So I volunteered you to sit at the table from two until four."

"Mommmmm! You didn't!"

Mrs. Leighton rolled her eyes. "I did. I'm sorry I didn't ask you first, but it seemed like the right thing to do and—"

"Oh, Mother! How could you?" Didn't her mother know that she didn't want to spend her entire weekend afternoon sitting at a bazaar selling brownies and sugar cookies?

"Just two hours, dear. For me?"

"All right," Lexi acquiesced ungraciously, "but don't let it happen again."

"Good. Thanks. Just go to the park and Elenore will give you the number of the assigned table. Someone from the last shift will be there when you arrive to give you instructions." She looked at her daughter's glum face. "It will be fun—every organization in town has a booth—the homemakers clubs, the literary clubs, even the people from the Symphony Ball are planning to have a booth. You'll see lots of people. Maybe you'll even have a good time."

"Maybe" was the operative word, Lexi thought to herself. *Maybe* she'd have a good time *if* she got through tonight without feeling too sorry for herself.

At six o'clock, Lexi began to prepare for her "date."

Mrs. Leighton knocked on her door and stepped into the room. "What are you wearing tonight? Something very special, I hope. Your dad has been looking forward to this all week."

"He has?"

"Sure. He told me the last time he was this excited about going out for dinner was the night he proposed to me."

"You're kidding, right?"

"Not at all." Mrs. Leighton stared at her daughter intently. "You're turning into a very lovely young woman. We're both proud of you."

"Then I'd better look spectacular tonight!" Lexi pawed through her closet in a sudden panic. "What should I wear?"

"You? The fashion expert—asking me?"

"I mean, should I be serious, prim and proper, exotic, preppy, what?"

"Be yourself. That's usually the most interesting."

"Myself. Hmmm." Lexi stared into her closet for a moment, squinting hard at the clothing. An idea was forming in her mind.

"Would you mind if I stitched that flouncy black taffeta skirt to the bottom of my black skinny knit sweater?"

"What?"

"I saw something like it in a magazine. Then it will be a one-piece dress with a dropped waistline and a pouffe skirt. I could put a big black bow in my hair and . . ." Lexi was off and running.

Mrs. Leighton, knowing better than to disturb her daughter's creative moods, threw her hands in the air. "For tonight. For your father."

By the time Mr. Leighton arrived home at seven, Lexi was standing in the doorway, tapping a black patent leather toe and glancing theatrically at her mother's borrowed watch.

"Look at you!" Mr. Leighton breathed.

"She's beeoootiiifulll!" Ben squealed on his way through the foyer to the kitchen.

"She certainly is. Are you sure she's my daughter?"

"You're too modest, Jim," Mrs. Leighton teased from the kitchen. "You'd better hurry. Your reservations are for seven-thirty."

It *was* rather special, Lexi thought, as her father escorted her into the family car, to have her very own evening with her dad. Maybe Minda *had* done her a favor by leaving her out. At least it had forced Lexi to think of something creative to do for the night.

But her gratitude to Minda didn't last long.

"I have some medication to drop off at Bill Long's place. His spaniel has an eye infection. They live out at 1500 Ridge Road. Do you mind if we swing by there? I'm sure we have time."

What could she say? "No, Dad, I don't want you to go to Longs because they live across the street from Hannafords?" Her father didn't even realize what he was asking.

"It would sure help him out to get this tonight. I'm worried about that pup's eye and—"

"Fine, Dad. No problem."

"Good girl."

Too good, Lexi decided as they pulled into the driveway across from the Hannafords. She should never have come.

Cars were driving in from every direction. Todd's old clunker was already in the driveway. Lexi wouldn't have felt more conspicuous if her hair had been on fire.

Tressa, Gina, and Mary Beth all came together. Lexi could see them staring and dipping their heads together to whisper their speculations.

"Hurry up, Dad!" she muttered to herself.

Just then her father strode out of the Longs' front door and waved her in.

"Me? In there?"

Mr. Leighton took three long strides to the car door. "Come and meet these people, Lexi. I want them to see what a beautiful daughter I have."

Nothing, absolutely nothing, except that plea

from her father, could have gotten her to move.

The taffeta rustled around her knees as she slid from the car. The dress looked good, she knew that—just like something from *Seventeen*. And her hair pulled back with a big bow made her look very sophisticated. At least she had that going for her as she made the million-mile trip from the car to the house.

Her heels clicked sharply on the concrete as she hurried, but still, she was not quick enough. A whistle rent the air, followed by a loud and brazen, "Well, hello, there!" Lexi turned and found herself looking directly into the green eyes of Jerry Randall.

He was as surprised as she.

He was driving his flashy sports car again. The chrome gleamed as though it had just left the showroom floor, and the motor purred as softly and smoothly as that of a contented kitten. The car was Jerry's pride and joy—no doubt about that. How, Lexi wondered, could a boy in high school afford a car like that?

Jerry's mouth worked a bit, as though he knew it was polite to speak, but no words left his mouth. Without a backward glance, Lexi hurried through the open door.

When she finally escaped the enthusiastic compliments of her father's friends, Lexi sank deep into the car seat and willed her father to hurry them away.

Mr. Leighton, unaware of her inner turmoil, sauntered slowly to the car, visiting with Mr. Long before he slid beneath the wheel.

"Well, we're off. Just in time for our reservations."

Just in time, all right, Lexi thought to herself. *Just in time to see Todd and Egg wander out of the house to look at something under the hood of Jerry's car.* Many sets of eyes followed her as she and her father drove slowly down the rode that curved by the Hannafords' house.

It was after midnight when Lexi and her father returned home. Mrs. Leighton was waiting up, her form shadowed by the reading lamp at her shoulder.

"I thought you two were lost!" was her greeting.

Mr. Leighton glanced at his watch. "Twelve-thirty already? We forgot about the time, didn't we, Lexi?"

"It was soooo good, Mom. The food was out of this world! And the waiter . . ."

" . . . was rather charmed by my daughter. I've never had such service."

"And there was a sign outside the restaurant advertising a band concert in the gazebo at the park."

"After that we drove around looking at the lights and . . ."

Mrs. Leighton stretched and rose from her chair. "Sounds like you two had a wonderful time. I hate to be the party-pooper here, but Lexi has another big day tomorrow—selling baked goods at the park."

"Ohhh," Lexi groaned, "I'd forgotten. Do I have to?"

"Need you ask?"

"I'd better get to bed, then. I suppose I'll need my rest in order to push pastries all afternoon. I can't think of anything more *boring*."

"G'night, Mom. Dad. And thanks."

"Your booth number is twenty-four. It's right next to the Symphony Ball booth." A heavy-set lady with gray hair and a pencil stuck behind her ear gave Lexi a little nudge toward a long aisle of booths. "Just go and tell whoever is at the booth that you're her replacement. It's been very busy, so I'm sure she'll be glad to see you."

Lexi had never seen such a hodge-podge of food and crafts in her life. Wooden rocking horses and clay pots, hand woven shawls and crab apple jelly, book-ends and oil paintings, stained glass and . . . Minda Hannaford!

There, in booth twenty-five, looking sour as a green apple, was Minda. A sign proclaiming "Symphony Ball Tickets—$25.00" fluttered over her head as she listlessly stacked little white tickets into piles. She glanced up at the startled utterance that slipped from Lexi's lips.

Minda's narrow face pinched tight in a scowl. "What are you doing here?"

Lexi gathered her wits about her and tilted her chin high in bravado. She'd gotten through last night—she could surely manage today.

"Selling baked goods for the church." She waved a hand in the direction of the brownies and cakes in booth twenty-four. "My mother asked me to do it."

"Yeah, well, so did mine. I knew it would be a dumb idea." And Minda gave her a look that said, "And now I'm sure of it." With that, she turned away, and Lexi knew she'd been dismissed as easily as if she were a mosquito on Minda's shoulder.

With an inward sigh, Lexi turned to her booth just as a woman in her late twenties came hurrying up.

"Are you my replacement?" Without waiting for a reply, the woman hurried on. "I'm Twila Wainright. I know I should stay for a few more minutes, but I have twin boys, and the babysitter just called to say that one of them had dropped my makeup down the toilet. I told her to call the plumber, but I suppose I'd better be there just in case. Those boys! What they won't think of next. If I'd known . . ." Mrs. Wainright rattled on like a pebble in an empty can, and Lexi, despite Minda's glares, could hardly keep from giggling.

"The coin box is on the floor, every item is baked fresh today, and, yes, we will take orders for pizelles, krumkake and all the other ethnic baked goods. Someone will be in to help you in two hours and, oh, my stars, I have to go. Nice to meet you . . ." Mrs. Wainright was gone in a flurry.

Lexi glanced at Minda from the corner of her eye. Her shoulders had a military rigidness and she purposefully kept her head and eyes averted. When a symphony patron stopped to buy a ticket, Minda managed to rearrange her chair so that her back faced Lexi. It was as though even looking at her was too much for Minda to bear.

"Please, God, I'm sorry she hates me. I didn't mean for this to happen. Help me not to return the hate." No wonder Binky thought their discussion about turning the other cheek had been strange. Today it seemed downright impossible.

It was easier to ignore Minda's icy disregard for her when people began to stop by the booth to make purchases. Lexi had almost forgotten her hostile boothmate when she heard a faint groan from the next table. Lexi spun around just as Minda crumpled over in her chair.

Her shoulders were hunched together, her head sunk deep between her shoulder blades as she gripped her abdomen in pain. Her pale cheeks matched the white sign fluttering overhead.

Lexi glanced to the right and left. Most of the crowd had moved to the far side of the park to watch two mimes examining the inside of an imaginary room. The booth on Minda's right had already sold out and closed for the day. They were virtually alone.

"Minda?" Lexi ventured.

Silence.

"Minda? Do you need help?" She pushed back her chair and moved hesitantly toward the booth. As much as Minda hated her, Lexi wondered if she would even allow her to help.

"You're white as a sheet!" The bleached, gray face that looked up at Lexi seemed like a caricature of the girl who'd turned her back on booth twenty-four. Minda was in obvious agony.

"Can I get you something? Water? A doctor? Should I call someone? Maybe I could get your mom or dad to—"

"No!" The word was staccato sharp. Minda straightened a bit and grimaced painfully as she did so. "I need to get home. I've got some medication there."

"Did you bring a car?"

"No. A lady from the Symphony Board dropped me off. I—ohhh!" Her body twisted with pain.

"Listen," Lexi began, "I've got my dad's car. I could drive you home if you think you could walk as far as the parking lot. If I drive close to the edge of the park, it wouldn't be too far." She wasn't sure Minda would accept her proposal. *She'd probably rather keel over and die in the park than let me help her*, Lexi thought. And from the way she looked, dying seemed imminent.

"I don't think . . ." she began. Then her arms tightened around her middle. "Okay."

Lexi glanced around. Mrs. Pierce was several booths away. Quickly she dashed toward the woman to explain her predicament. Even before Mrs. Pierce could rise from her chair, Lexi was back at Minda's side. Gently, she touched the girl's shoulder. "Can you straighten up?"

"No." The girl's voice was tight and raspy with discomfort. "Just steer me in the right direction and hurry."

Even in this condition, Minda was boss, Lexi observed, but she didn't argue. The pair stumbled awkwardly toward the edge of the park, stopping every minute or so as a wave of pain seemed to overtake Minda. When it would pass, they would resume their trek.

Lexi helped Minda to a bench and ran for the car. She could feel patches of nervous perspiration making her T-shirt cling to her back. What was wrong with Minda? She'd never seen anyone act like this. She glanced back at the forlorn figure on the park bench. Minda didn't seem so formidable now.

"Can you ride?" Lexi worried as she helped Minda into the car. "It's bound to be bumpy."

"Do I have a choice?" Minda asked weakly.

She must be better than she looks, Lexi observed.

Some of the old spit and fire was coming back.

Minda was silent on the trip to the Hannafords', except for an occasional groan of anguish as the car hit a dip in the road.

"I didn't know how bumpy city streets could be," Lexi muttered. "My dad's going to have to get the shocks checked on this thing."

"Owwwww!"

"Maybe we should just go to the hospital, Minda. It's not all that far and—"

"No!" Minda straightened up for a milli-second before crumpling back onto the seat. "I told you. I've got medication at home."

It was useless to argue. That was obvious. Minda's jaw was jutting forward in her usual unrelenting way. Despite her misery she was determined to get home. Lexi stared straight ahead and pressed her foot to the gas.

There were no cars in Hannafords' garage. Lexi pulled in close to the house, flicked off the ignition, and ran around to the passenger side to help Minda from the car.

"Here, lean on me. I think I could carry you if I had to. I'm pretty strong. Now, one step at a time." She coached Minda into the house, through the spacious foyer, and into the large formal living room.

Despite her concentration on her unexpected patient, Lexi couldn't help but notice the Hannaford home. The only rooms she had ever seen that were prettier were on the pages of her mother's *Home Beautiful* magazines. The foyer had high, uniquely shaped stained glass windows in mauve and pale blue. Those colors carried over into the vast expanse of pale blue carpet and delicate French provincial mauve furniture. Even the fresh flowers on the coffee table were mauve and blue.

But she didn't have much time for sightseeing as Minda doubled up with another pain.

"My medication. In the kitchen. On the window ledge over the sink."

Lexi hurried through the formal dining room and into a vast oak and chrome kitchen. The medication was where Minda had said it was, in a small brown container. After taking the glass that was sitting on the counter and filling it with tap water, Lexi hurried back to Minda.

"Here. How many do you need?"

"Two. Can you open the bottle?"

It was tempting to read the side of the bottle to get some clue as to the cause of Minda's suffering, but Lexi resisted the temptation. Her father always said that stealing information that you weren't supposed to have was no better than stealing more tangible things. She set the bottle on the table with the written directions facing the other way.

"Do you need a blanket? I could get a pillow and—"

"Are you kidding? And mess up the house? My mother would kill me." Minda began to struggle to her feet. "If I can just get to my room."

"Here, let me help you."

Minda gave her an odd stare. Lexi could see that whatever was in the medication was already beginning to give Minda some relief.

"You've helped me too much already."

"I don't mind. Here, just lean on me."

Unwillingly, Minda allowed Lexi to circle her waist with her arm and lead her into the bedroom.

Minda's bedroom was even more spectacular than the living room, Lexi decided. It was twice as large as her room at home. The carpet was a pale pink, like a whorl of cotton candy, and the drapes and bedspread were a deep, rich cherry color. There was a television, a video player, a stereo with compact disc player, and a collection of tapes on the bookshelf that lined one wall. Minda's French provincial phone and her elaborate clock radio sat on the nightstand next to her bed. There was even a tiny refrigerator built into the twenty-foot-long bookcase. *Enough to boggle a person's mind,* Lexi thought.

"You could get sent to your room and never want to come out!" Lexi blurted. Then she blushed to a pink as deep as the bedspread. "Sorry. That's none of my business."

Surprisingly, Minda smiled. "I know. It's happened dozens of times." Weakly she lay back against the cherry-colored pillows and closed her eyes.

"Are you all right?"

"I'm so tired." Minda's eyes fluttered open and she looked at Lexi. "I'm just going to close my eyes for a minute. Don't go away, okay?" And almost immediately, Minda was asleep.

Lexi shifted her weight awkwardly from one foot to the other and stared down at her unexpected charge. Here she was, the night after the celebrated party, watching over her archenemy.

Now what?

Chapter Five

Lexi stood awkwardly in the center of the room for a moment, wondering what to do next. It would serve Minda right if she just walked out. Lexi glanced longingly at the door and then at the pale, pinched form on the bed. *Hurt her!* all her instincts cried. *Make her pay for everything she's done.*

Then the words that she'd struggled with during family devotions came back to her. "Do not take revenge on someone who wrongs you. If anyone slaps you on the right cheek, let him slap your left cheek too."

Turn the other cheek.

Lexi moved toward the bed. Minda slept soundly, a slender arm thrown across her forehead, her pale hair spread over the pillow. She was prettier, Lexi observed, when she was sleeping, when all anger and nastiness had been shed. "All right, Minda," Lexi whispered, more to herself than to the sleeping girl. "Here's my other cheek. Let's see if you slap this one, too." Moving to the far side of the room, Lexi situated herself in a cherry-colored watered-silk chair and waited.

Nearly a half hour later, she heard a faint rustling sound from the bed.

Though Minda's skin was pale and translucent as skimmed milk, the pinched, hurting look was gone. Lexi stood up, waiting awkwardly, wondering what to do next. *Oh, God, help! I don't like this and I don't like her!*

Finally Lexi managed to ask, "How are you feeling?"

"Better." Minda's gaze roamed curiously across Lexi's face. "Why are you here?"

"You asked me to stay." *Didn't she even realize what a struggle it had been to stay?*

"I know. But I didn't think you would."

"I was worried about you. You seemed awfully sick. I thought you might need help."

"Yeah?" Minda weighed Lexi's words. "Thanks."

"You're welcome."

Lexi stood in the center of the room feeling very awkward and out of place. Why didn't Minda explain? Or at least say *something*!

Finally, Lexi asked, "Do you think I should call a doctor? I know you didn't want me to before, but—"

"Nah, it's just my ulcers acting up. I have a doctor's appointment on Friday. I can tell him then."

"Ulcers? Aren't you kind of young for—"

Minda's face grew grim. "I thought so too, but I guess not."

What could bother Minda so much that she had

ulcers? Lexi wondered as she glanced around. How could anyone find things to worry about in this marvelous cherry-colored room full of any girl's dreams? Then she remembered the overheard conversation between Minda and her mother. This cherry confection of a room couldn't help Minda with that.

"Maybe I should be going," Lexi began, eager to be away from Minda's pain-washed eyes.

Minda bit down on her lower lip as if in deep concentration. When she spoke, the words dumbfounded Lexi. "Maybe you could stay awhile? We could make some toast or something."

It was Lexi's turn to ask "Why?"

Minda's face grew hard. "Never mind. I should never have asked."

"No, that's not it. I could stay if you really wanted me to. But why do you want me? I mean, it's not like we've gotten along or anything, and last night—"

"Last night!" Minda spat. "What a disaster." Her face registered some of the pained expression she had worn at the park. "I suppose I should have asked you to the party . . ." Her voice trailed away.

Lexi felt tears well up in her eyes, but she didn't let them fall. She wouldn't let Minda know how much it had hurt to be the only one of her friends and acquaintances left out. She wouldn't allow Minda that satisfaction. "I had other plans."

"I know."

Lexi glanced at her in surprise. "You do?"

Minda's expression was a mixture of confusion and anger. "I thought I could show you that you couldn't walk out on Hi-Five and get away with it. You made a fool of me in front of my friends." Minda's eyes narrowed, and Lexi could see sparks of hatred, frustration, and anger. "Instead, you were the talk of the party."

Lexi's dumbfounded expression brought a twisted half smile to Minda's lips.

"Todd and Egg and Jerry saw you over at the Longs'. So did Tressa and the others. All they could talk about was how great you looked—how sophisticated. Tressa went on and on about your dress." Minda looked crestfallen. "It all blew up in my face. I wanted people to know that I'd left you out on purpose—and then Jerry and Tressa saw you with this good looking older guy, and everyone figured you'd turned down the party to go out with him."

Lexi stared at the angry girl for a long moment before a bubble of laughter burst from her lips. "But that was my *father*!"

Minda's eyes grew round. "Your father? You went out in a sophisticated black dress with your *father*? Tressa said you were dressed like a fashion model."

Lexi smiled. "I made that dress."

"You *made* it?" The anger changed into undisguised awe in Minda's voice. "Really?"

"Sure. I do it all the time."

Minda rolled over on her side and stared at Lexi. Just when Lexi thought she'd pop with curiosity, Minda said, "Want that toast?"

Becoming more and more curious about what Minda would come up with next, Lexi nodded, then followed her to the kitchen.

She watched Minda move around the kitchen while the questions multiplied in her head. When Minda had toasted and buttered a stack of toast and sprinkled it with cinnamon and sugar, she thrust it in front of Lexi.

"I'm making hot chocolate too. It settles pretty well in my stomach," she announced frankly.

Lexi just nodded, not knowing what to say. She picked up a piece of toast and chewed on the edge. Minda pulled up a stool across from her and did the same. It was quiet except for the occasional clink of a mug. Then, just as Lexi was growing somewhat accustomed to the silence, it was broken by a car pulling into the driveway. An expression passed over Minda's face that Lexi could not identify. Panic? Fear?

The door slammed and Mrs. Hannaford came bursting into the room. She wore a crisp linen suit and more diamonds than Lexi had ever seen. Every finger flashed and gleamed with light. She flung her leather purse onto the table and proceeded to verbally tear Minda's father to shreds, regardless of Minda or her company.

Lexi slid quickly off the stool. "I probably should be going now. Thank you for the lunch."

Minda nodded absently. Her eyes had taken on the same glazed look they'd worn when her stomach was hurting in the park.

Then she turned and looked directly at Lexi. "Come again?" As she said it, Minda seemed startled by her own words.

Turn the other cheek. "If you want me to," Lexi responded halfheartedly as she ducked through the door and into the sunlight. The last words she heard as she slipped through the front door were those of Mrs. Hannaford.

"Look at what you've done to this kitchen! Crumbs everywhere. You're no better than your father. Lazy, thoughtless . . ."

Lexi's lips hardened into a thin line. How had she ever gotten involved in this, she wondered. After all, she didn't even *like* the Hannafords!

As much as she willed it otherwise, Minda stayed on Lexi's mind for the rest of the day. That was why it didn't surprise her when she saw Minda walking up the sidewalk to her front porch.

From the corner of her eye, Lexi saw Ben peer out the front window, and seeing Minda, he skittered away up the stairs. *Maybe I should do the same,* Lexi thought to herself.

Still, when the doorbell rang, she moved to answer it.

Minda, looking pale and nervous, shifted her weight from heel to toe and back again as she stood in the doorway.

Lexi had no desire to invite her in, but the manners her mother had drilled into her since childhood left her no choice. "Come in?"

"For a minute" Minda stepped past Lexi and into the house.

"You forgot this." Minda opened her hand to reveal a tube of lip gloss and dropped it into Lexi's hand.

Lexi stared at the familiar tube. "It must have fallen out of the pocket of my blouse. Thanks."

"You're welcome." Instead of turning to leave as

Lexi expected, Minda remained bolted to the foyer floor.

"I'm having lemonade . . ." Lexi finally began.

"I'd love some." Minda unrooted herself and strolled into the living room, leaving Lexi no choice but to follow her.

Keeping a wary eye on her visitor, Lexi poured two tall glasses of lemonade and added a twist of lemon to each glass.

"Feeling better?" she finally inquired.

"Yes." Minda took a dainty sip. "As soon as the medication starts to work I—" Her eyes widened and Lexi glanced backward over her shoulder to see what it was that had startled her visitor.

Ben was sitting on the steps, a teddy bear in one hand and rubber snake in the other.

"Go put your snake away, Ben. Maybe our company doesn't like snakes."

"Snakes," Ben echoed and dangled the thing by its tail.

Lexi turned to Minda and explained apologetically, "My dad bought him that because he was so terrified of snakes. He'd go berserk if he saw one on television or in the garden. Dad thought it would make him less afraid." Lexi chuckled wryly. "It worked too well. Now he's absolutely fearless—and that dumb thing turns up in my bed and my shoes and—"

"You mean he puts it there?"

"Sure. You know how brothers are. He—"

"But he's not like other brothers," Minda pointed out. "He's . . . you know."

Lexi shrugged. "It doesn't seem to have affected his sense of humor."

Minda was staring hard at Ben, and he was returning the gaze with equal intensity. Then, in a move Lexi wouldn't have predicted in a million years, Ben slid himself down the last of the steps and moved straight toward Minda.

"See?" He held out the rubber snake. "Don't be 'fraid. It's okay. Can't hurt." He crooned out the words that his father had told him. "It's okay."

Minda glanced from the snake to Ben's concerned face and then to Lexi. "He's trying to make me not scared of snakes!"

"Sure. You're a good boy, aren't you, Ben?"

"Good boy," he echoed. The rubber snake slithered out of his hand as he spied Lexi's lemonade sitting on the end table. Before she could stop him, he'd dropped the bear, too, and was slurping up Lexi's entire glass. He tilted his head back to get the final drop.

Minda began to giggle.

"What's so funny?" Lexi groused. "Now I have to get another glass for myself."

"Him." Minda pointed at Ben's receding back as he meandered into the kitchen. "He's just like a . . . kid."

"He is a kid."

"But a real one, not . . ." Even Minda had the grace to look embarrassed. "I didn't mean it like that. He's just not as . . . weird as I expected him to be."

"Thanks, I think." Lexi's head was beginning to throb. What did Minda want here, anyway?

"You're really different, aren't you?" Minda

asked with a breath of amazement in her voice. She sat staring at Lexi as if she'd just landed from outer space.

"Hmmm . . . just what I've always wanted to be, 'different.' "

"Oh, I didn't mean *bad* different, exactly," Minda went on. "Just *different* different."

"That makes it all perfectly clear." Lexi couldn't help but smile. Minda couldn't seem to say anything without offending her. It was almost becoming funny.

"Like when you helped me home from the park. You didn't have to do that."

"But you were sick."

"And I've been rotten to you. Why didn't you just leave me there?"

Lexi thought about the story of the good Samaritan and how he'd been unable to leave someone ill and in trouble by the side of the road, but it seemed too difficult to explain that to Minda, so she just sat quietly.

"It's because you're a Christian, isn't it?"

"That's part of it."

"Do you really believe in all that stuff?"

Minda's frank question drove a wedge of alarm into Lexi's heart.

Minda's jaw jutted forward defensively. "Maybe Jesus was a big deal once—in the olden days—but not now. Who talks to God now, anyway? Seems like a real waste of time to me."

"Why?"

"It's pretty obvious, isn't it? I mean, if there actually is a God at all, why does He let bad things happen? If He's so great and wonderful and powerful like everyone says, why doesn't He *fix* things?"

"What kind of things?" Lexi remained seated, her back straight and long, her head tilted ever so slightly to one side.

Minda rose and began to prowl restlessly about the room. Her hand fluttered lightly over the picture frames on the sofa table, across the photo album on the seat of a chair. When she finally sat down again, it was with the tentativeness of a butterfly landing.

"Just things. Bad things. Hurtful things. Things that should never happen."

Lexi sensed the turmoil in Minda and remained silent.

Minda picked at a stray thread on the couch, her fingers trembling. "God is a fraud." She challenged Lexi with her gaze. Then the defiant expression faltered. "If there's a God, why does He let my parents fight all the time?"

Lexi felt as though she'd been punched in the stomach.

"God!" Minda continued, her anger building. "Big Daddy up in the sky, right? He'll take care of us, make it all right. That's a laugh. You Christians are a bunch of jerks, that's all—believing garbage like that! It makes me so mad sometimes that I—"

"It's okay to be mad." Lexi's soft words stopped Minda midstream.

"What?"

"About your parents fighting. It's okay to be mad. I would be."

A flicker of interest brightened Minda's angry, tear-filled eyes. "I thought you Christians couldn't get mad at God."

Lexi smiled. "We have emotions just like you do."

"If God was worth anything at all, He wouldn't let this happen to me. My parents used to love each other. I know they did. They wouldn't have gotten married if they didn't. But now—"

"And you think God made them quit loving each other?"

Minda looked confused. "I don't know. I just get so"—her voice quavered—"so angry."

"You can be angry at what's happening without being mad at God."

Minda looked blank. "I don't get it."

"God didn't send you problems. Why would He? He loves us—all of us. There's no reason for Him to be looking for revenge or anything like that."

Minda gave her an even more doubtful glance, and Lexi hurried to explain herself.

"God isn't the bad guy in all of this." She chose her words as carefully as she could. "Dad says that we live in a sinful, messy world and that God is our example of what's good and right—and He can give us His strength when we run out of our own. That's where faith and forgiveness come in."

Minda glanced theatrically at the ceiling. "So where is He now? Out to lunch?" She flung herself backward in her chair. "What do you know about it anyway, Miss Goody-Two-Shoes? Nothing's wrong with you."

Just then Ben came jogging through the living room again, his distinctive gait making him bounce like a rubber ball. He stopped in front of Lexi and gave her cheek a pat.

"Hungry."

"There are cookies on the table. You can reach them."

He nodded and resumed his half-skip, half-slide run through the room.

When he disappeared, Lexi looked up and stared straight into Minda's eyes. When she spoke, her words were thick with emotion.

"I was pretty mad at God for a while myself."

Minda didn't speak, but a glimmer of understanding lit her features.

"I hated God too, Minda. I couldn't understand why He'd let Ben be born so . . . hurt."

"And now you understand?" Minda stared at the door through which Ben had disappeared.

"No."

"Then are you still mad?"

"No." Her brow furrowed. "But I don't think anymore that God decided Ben would be a Down's baby. For a while I thought that God was punishing us for something—maybe something bad that I or one of my parents had done—but I don't believe that now. I think Ben's handicap just happened—like earthquakes or disease happen. Germs don't pick certain people to make sick, and earthquakes don't decide where they'll hit. It just happens."

"And people's marriages break up?" Minda snapped her fingers, "Just like that?"

"I guess so."

"So why doesn't God stop it? Why doesn't He make Ben normal?" Minda demanded. "It's a crummy system, if you ask me."

Lexi smiled wanly. "I think people lots smarter than us have asked that question. My dad says that sometimes there aren't any answers—just more questions."

"Well, I don't get it," Minda concluded. "What good is God, anyway? If He refuses to fix things, why bother with Him?"

Lexi paused for a long moment. When she spoke her voice held a note of confusion. "It's hard to explain this, but after I got over being mad at Him, I finally figured it out."

"You figured out what God is for?"

Lexi nodded. "I think so." Her brow furrowed even more deeply. "He's not the one who sends trouble— or magically bails us out. He's the one who is on our side all the time the trouble is going on."

"What good is that?" Minda scoffed.

"What good is a best friend?" Lexi countered.

"Huh?"

"It's a little like that," Lexi struggled to explain. "Once you realize you aren't angry anymore, you find out that it's partly because He's been there all along—helping you to be stronger and braver than you thought you ever could. He makes the trouble easier to handle, Minda, but He doesn't always take it away. Ben is still retarded, but I can accept that now."

"It's all too weird for me," Minda announced. "Way too weird." And with a lightning change of mood, the old, confident Minda was back. She flipped her hair from her eyes. "Anyway, I just wanted to bring back your lipstick, not get into some big, stupid conversation about something or Someone who doesn't even exist."

Lexi nodded, her head spinning at Minda's swift

mood swing. "Thanks for bringing back the lipstick."

"Yeah." Minda moved toward the door. She turned a worried look on Lexi. "Listen, this God stuff—it's just between you and me, right?"

"Right."

"Okay . . . I just don't want anyone to know I'd talk about this junk." And she was gone.

For a long time Lexi stood quietly, her head against the open door. Staring at the deepening shadows, she wondered what strange twist her life would take next.

Chapter Six

"There's Todd," Lexi observed as she and Jennifer left the main door of the mall. "Looks like he's having car trouble."

Todd was hunched over the hood of the old coupe, his shoulders drooping disconsolately.

"You go cheer him up," Jennifer suggested. "I've got to get home. Maybe he'll throw your bike in the back and give you a ride." An impish grin brightened her features. "Lucky you."

"Very funny," Lexi retorted. She and Jennifer had spent the afternoon looking for summer sales—and an air-conditioned spot to spend a hot afternoon. "See you later."

Jennifer saluted, swung her leg over the seat of her ten-speed and sped away, her plastic shopping bags all dangling over one shoulder and flopping against her back.

When Lexi reverted her eyes to Todd, he was still in the same odd position, hunched over the car, his head hung low. What was wrong?

"Todd? Are you okay?" She approached him cautiously, unsure of herself in his presence.

His head came up with a sharp jerk. Lexi was shocked by the miserable look in his eyes.

"Are you having car trouble?" she murmured, though already positive that mere car trouble wouldn't cause the hurting expression on his face.

An abrupt burst of humorless laughter escaped him. "Car trouble? You might call it that."

The tone of his voice frightened her. Todd was as even-tempered a person as she'd ever met. This angry, lashing tone shocked her.

Immediately he read the concern in her eyes. "Hey, I'm sorry. I didn't mean to snap like that. It's just that . . . oh, never mind."

"Tell me." Lexi propped herself against the hood of the car and crossed her arms in a determined gesture. "I'm waiting."

He smiled and a little touch of humor finally lit his eyes. "Bossy, aren't you?"

"Crabby, aren't *you?*"

This time he gave a full-fledged grin. "Yeah. And I'm sorry. It's just been a rotten day."

"So what happened?"

"I went into my brother's garage this afternoon as usual. I had a couple little jobs lined up to do for guys from the high school and I wanted to change the air filter on my own car."

"And?"

"And when I walked in, my brother nearly took my head off."

"Why?"

"Because he went through my tools, and there's another wrench missing." Todd kicked at the pavement with the toe of his hightopped tennis shoe. "One of his this time—one I'd borrowed to replace my own missing one."

"Ouch."

"Yeah." He stared forlornly across the parking lot. "I drove out here to the supply house to see how much it would cost to replace Mike's set of crescent wrenches."

"Don't they have them?" Lexi wondered.

"Sure they do. But the quality precision tools that Mike has are even more expensive than I'd first thought. I couldn't even begin to afford the stuff I've lost!"

"But did *you* actually lose it?" Lexi questioned. "I can't imagine you being that careless."

Todd shrugged. "I didn't either, but the stuff is missing. Nobody else has the problem. Maybe I've got too much on my mind. Between Camp Courage and softball and all the other things I'm involved in, I just don't pay enough attention at the shop." He gave a humorless chuckle. "But I've become extra careful now. Mike said that if things didn't quit disappearing, he was going to have a long talk with our parents."

"He hasn't told them yet?"

"No. We both know how disappointed they'd be in me." Todd raked his fingers through his hair. "I just keep trying to remember how I handled those tools. I can't recall putting them back, so that must mean I just laid them somewhere to get picked up or driven away."

Lexi hoisted herself to the high riding bumper of the old car and allowed her bare legs to dangle over the side. The sun-warmed metal felt hot and smooth against her skin. "Maybe that's it. Maybe someone else is picking them up and putting them somewhere."

Todd shook his head. "I've asked the other guys, and they don't know anything about it." His eyebrows furrowed together across the bridge of his nose. "If there were any *new* guys, it might be different, but all Mike's employees have been working there at least four years. They wouldn't pull any funny business now."

"How about people hanging around the shop? Anyone new?" This smacked of a little mystery. Mysteries had always intrigued Lexi.

"No. He has his regular customers plus drop-ins—besides, very few people get back into the work area. Most people don't like to hang out where everything is greasy. They stay up front in the customer service area. Mike lets some of the guys from school use the hoist to work on their own cars, but it's been the same group for two or three years."

"I see your problem," Lexi murmured. Pursing her lips thoughtfully, she said, "But I just don't think you're the careless type, Todd. If those tools are disappearing, I think they're having help."

"Thank you, Miss Detective, for your vote of confidence!"

Lexi grinned, stiffened her legs, and slid off the bumper of the car. "Could we go to your brother's garage and just look around?"

"For clues, you mean?" Todd was making fun of her now.

Her chin came up defiantly. "Maybe, maybe not.

You aren't figuring this out on your own, you know. What can it hurt if I look around?"

His shoulders sagged again, just as they had been when she'd first approached him. "You're right. You can't do any worse than I am."

"Don't be so down, Todd. At least Mike knows you aren't *stealing* them!"

"True, but it's almost as bad. Being irresponsible is really frowned upon in my family. You know my mother—Mrs. Efficiency. I could be grounded for weeks if Mike goes to them."

That statement left a sinking feeling in Lexi's stomach. What would *she* do without Todd around to count on for support and friendship? Suddenly, she knew it was very important to all of them to discover what was going on at Mike's garage.

"Come on, let's go to the garage. I want to check it out just in case my bike needs some work." She dusted her hands on the fronts of her thighs and tried to look brisk and businesslike.

"Good try, Lexi. But all you want to do is snoop." He angled his head toward where her bike was parked. "Roll that thing over here and I'll throw it in the trunk. Maybe letting you loose in the garage is a good idea. Maybe in my absent-mindedness I put a box wrench in a flower pot, who knows?"

At least Todd was smiling again, Lexi observed as they drove toward Mike's garage. He obviously felt terrible about disappointing his brother—and more worried yet about his parents' response. But heavy metal objects *didn't* just walk away. And maybe a couple did accidentally get left on top of the engines of cars, but not so many as to force Todd to work all summer without pay to compensate for them! There had to be a reason, and Lexi wanted to help Todd discover what it was.

As they pulled up, Mike's garage was a hub of activity. Every stall held a vehicle in some stage of disrepair. There were a group of boys working on an old clunker up on the hoist. Lexi recognized a few from the musical but couldn't remember their names. Jerry Randall was the only really familiar face.

"Slumming?" Jerry drawled when he saw Lexi and Todd enter the shop.

"Are you?" she responded back. She wished Jerry's tongue wasn't so sharp and hurtful. He could be nice if only he chose to be.

Jerry gave her a confused look and turned back to the car on which he and his friend were working.

Mike Winston sauntered over to greet them. "Hiya."

"Hi, yourself," Todd responded. "Lexi wanted to take a closer look at the shop."

"Maybe she can find my box wrenches," Mike growled meaningfully. He exchanged a glance with his brother that Lexi could only interpret as a warning. Her heart sank. Todd really was in trouble with his much-admired older brother.

"Hey, Mike!" Jerry yelled, interrupting the nervous energy flowing between the threesome, "have you got a set of ratchet wrenches we can use over here?"

Mike tipped his head toward Todd. "Let them use yours." His eyes narrowed. "And make sure they get put back where they belong."

Todd slowly moved toward the workbench where he kept his tools. He pulled open a drawer and dug inside. When he looked up, his eyes were wide and worried. "It's not here, Mike. The set isn't in here."

"What?" Mike and Lexi crossed the floor to where Todd stood, and stared down into the drawer. Lexi couldn't recognize a single tool in there except for the screwdriver and hammer, but both Todd and Mike seemed to know what was missing.

"I put it in there. I know I did."

"And it evaporated? Come on, Todd. Shape up. Where are they?" Mike's voice was a warning rumble.

"I don't know! I would've sworn that they were in—"

"Don't give me this again! How many times have I told you not to leave stuff lying around? Yesterday I picked up half a dozen things you'd left out. What makes you think you can get by with that? My other men don't . . ." Mike's voice was escalating, and the other people in the garage had stopped what they were doing and begun to listen.

Lexi wanted to shrivel up and disappear. She could understand Mike's anger. Todd was supposed to be doing a job, and he didn't seem to be living up to it. Still, she just couldn't believe that Todd was as careless as everyone seemed to think. He wasn't thoughtless in any other area of his life. Why this one?

"I can't afford to have you around here if you don't shape up, Todd," Mike was saying. His voice echoed through the cavern of the room and shuddered off the steel rafters. "I'll give you till the end of the month to shape up. If things are still disappearing after that"—Mike's voice lowered, but it seemed to echo even louder throughout the room—"then you're the one who has to disappear. I won't hang on to an employee who keeps losing things. Brother or not, shape up or you're out." With that, Mike spun on his heels and stalked angrily toward his office.

Todd seemed frozen to the spot. Lexi glanced around. The mechanics had gone back to work, pretending self-consciously that they hadn't heard the exchange between the brothers. The group of boys had all wisely slipped away, knowing full well that they were present as a result of Mike's good nature— and his disposition had momentarily taken a turn for the worse.

"Todd"—she reached out and laid a comforting hand on his sleeve—"I'm so sorry."

He shook his head and turned toward her, a sad look creasing his face. "Mike's right, Lexi. He's put up with this a lot longer than he would have if I hadn't been his brother. Maybe I'll start using a checklist or something. I know I used those ratchets last night. I thought I put them away. But it was late and I was in a hurry . . ." He shook his head and gave Lexi a weak smile. "I thought I'd be at least fifty years older before my mind started to go, Lexi." He grabbed her arm. "Come on, I'd better get you home before I forget the way!"

The trip to Leightons' was long and silent as they both pondered the mystery of the missing tools—and what would happen to Todd if his parents found out what was going on.

Chapter Seven

"I know, I know, 'How did I get to be sixteen and never learn how to swim?' Don't ask. Just don't ask." Egg wore an anguished expression that clashed with the wildly cheerful Hawaiian print of his swim trunks. "All I know is that I don't want to learn now."

"Lexi was a lifeguard, Egg," Binky assured her brother. "And Todd's on the swim team. If they can't teach you, no one can!"

"Exactly what I just said. No one can! I don't want to learn." Egg did a gangly sidestep that took him one step away from the edge of the pool.

"If he doesn't want to do it, why make him?" Lexi added. "He looks scared to death."

"Because my parents said they might take us on a canoe trip next summer if Egg learned to swim," Binky announced. "And besides that, everyone swims around here."

That much was true, Lexi decided. The municipal pool was a wild splash of activity, and every square inch of concrete surrounding the water was covered with beach towels and swimsuit clad bodies.

"I'll get a tan. You guys swim," Egg pleaded. "Please?"

"Just get wet today. You have to start somewhere. Maybe even dip your face in the water—just for a second." Todd took Egg by the arm and steered him toward the pool. Egg's gangly arms and legs were no match for Todd's muscular strength as he found himself being propelled toward the water.

"Should I go help him?" Binky wondered. "Egg looks pretty worried."

"He'll be fine. Todd won't force him to do anything he doesn't want to do." Lexi smoothed her own towel on the space she'd claimed and lay down in the sun.

"Yeah. You're right." Binky plopped down beside her. "Todd's too nice a guy to just dump him in. That's what Jerry Randall did—and that's why Egg is so scared of the water. Jerry just stood and laughed. When he finally realized that Egg was actually having trouble, Jerry had to call a lifeguard to pull Egg out."

"Good old Jerry," Lexi muttered. Neither she nor Todd had felt like facing him since he'd witnessed that embarrassing exchange at Mike's garage.

"How about 'good old Minda'?" Binky retorted. "Here she comes with her bikini brigade."

Lexi opened one eye. Minda, Tressa, and Mary Beth were sauntering toward them, stepping on beach towels, blankets, and bodies that got in their way.

"I think we'd better get out of here," Binky whispered urgently.

"Why?"

"Because this is where the Hi-Fivers usually sit. We're in their spot."

"But we were here first!"

"That doesn't matter. Everybody knows that the Hi-Five likes it here."

"I didn't."

"That's because you're new."

"And that's the reason I'm staying put."

Binky gave a low groan. "Don't do this to me, Lexi. I hate scenes."

"There won't be a scene."

"When Minda sees you in her spot? Hah!"

Lexi wasn't as confident as she would have liked Binky to believe, but this was a public pool. She and her friends could sit wherever they wanted. She hoped.

"What's this?" Lexi recognized Tressa's voice and had a feeling it was Tressa's toe prodding her shoulder. "Someone is in our spot."

Lexi willed her eyes to stay closed. The toe poked even harder. She rolled to her back and opened her eyes. Tressa was looking at her with the same interest she might show in a bug under a microscope.

"Are you talking to me?" Lexi inquired innocently. She could see Binky's eyes growing wide with wonder and dismay.

"You're the one in our spot."

"I'm sorry. Did you have it marked?" Lexi blinked slowly and lazily. Her eyes held a hint of challenge.

"Marked? You want markers? Ask anyone here"—Tressa flung her arm wide to encompass everyone at the pool—"and they'll tell you who belongs here."

"Funny," Lexi murmured with a yawn. "If it's

that important, you'd think someone would have erected a monument."

Binky choked back a bubble of laughter.

"Just what is that supposed to mean? We always—"

"Come on, Tressa," Minda, who had been silent, broke in. "There's a spot opening up over there."

"But we always—"

"Don't sound like a broken record, Tressa. Come on." With that, Minda spun around on her sandal-shod heel and stalked toward the vacant space. Too dumbfounded to speak, Tressa followed. Mary Beth glanced from Lexi to Minda and back again before she finally joined her friends.

"How'd you do that?" Binky gasped.

"Do what?"

"Make the Hi-Fivers go away from this spot."

"I didn't make anyone do anything. You heard Minda. Another spot opened up."

"But they don't do—"

Lexi was glad to see Todd and a slightly damp Egg returning. She didn't want to go into her encounters with Minda. Still, today had proved a point: Minda now knew that Lexi refused to be walked on again, used and abused like a discarded rug.

"It's a start," Todd was telling Egg. "Tomorrow we'll get you into the shallow end of the pool and play a little tag. Pretty soon you'll wonder why you hated the water."

"It's all babies in that end of the pool," Egg groused. "I'll feel like a fool."

"Not as much as you will if you fall into the water and have to be rescued by someone half your size,"

Todd retorted cheerfully. He turned to Lexi. "Did Tressa and Minda say something to you?"

"Not much," Lexi answered quickly. She didn't want Binky to rehash the scene.

"Minda, quiet?" Egg asked, incredulous. "That's strange. Must be trouble on the home front again."

"What do you mean by that?"

He shrugged. "Oh, nothing. Sometimes my mom gets calls to clean at the Hannafords' when their regular cleaning lady is on vacation. Mom just says it's not a very nice household. I don't think Mr. and Mrs. Hannaford get along very well."

"That's gossip, Egg," Binky warned, chirping like Egg's out-of-body conscience. "Mom doesn't want you repeating things."

"I know. But I'll bet you anything it's true."

"Still, you shouldn't say it."

That seemed to silence Egg for the moment, and the four of them lay sprawled in the sun like so many pieces of bacon on a griddle.

Lexi was the first to stand up. "I think I'd better get going. I promised Mom I'd do some things around the house."

"Have time for a malt at the Hamburger Shack?" Todd asked.

"Not today. Thanks anyway. Don't leave just because I am." She slid her feet into thongs and wrapped her towel around her slim waist.

"See you later," Egg mumbled.

Lexi grinned over the top of Egg's head at Todd. "Right." As she turned to leave, Minda's intent stare startled her. Something was going on in that pale blond head, Lexi decided, but she was at a loss to know what it might be.

Lexi was deep into watering the flowerbeds when Minda arrived at the front step.

"Hello." Lexi glanced up, startled.

Minda remained silent.

"Can I help you?"

Minda walked to where Lexi was standing and stared down at the flowerbed where the marigolds were just coming into their own in a riot of rusts and yellows.

"I like flowers."

Lexi blinked at the unexpected statement. "Me too. Except when I have to weed the flowerbeds."

"Our gardener does that."

"I see." That put a stop to their conversation, and both girls stood awkwardly as if waiting for the other to speak.

Just then, Ben came barreling out of the house and onto the porch. He wore his favorite plastic fireman's hat on his head and, as usual, had the vacuum cleaner hose looped around his shoulders.

"Fire! Fire! Vrrrooooooommmm!" He raced around the porch twice and then came to a grinding halt in front of Minda. "Hi."

She looked at him doubtfully. "Hi, yourself."

"Trucks?" he inquired and held out his hand.

"What does he want?" Minda hissed.

"He wants to show you his trucks."

"Where are they?"

"In his room."

"Should he be doing this?"

"He must remember you. He usually doesn't invite people to see his trucks unless he really likes them."

"He doesn't?" Minda, unable to resist being one of a select few, hesitantly followed Ben into the house.

Grinning to herself, Lexi finished watering the flowers, carefully looped the garden hose around its carrier, and kicked off her damp sandals. Inside the house, she could hear Ben and Minda having a conversation.

"What's this?" Minda would ask.

"Heavy-duty truck," Ben answered.

"And what's this?"

"Pickup."

"Then, do you know what this is called?"

"Sports car."

"Is this a test?" Lexi peeked around the door at the pair on the rug. A startled Minda glanced toward the doorway.

Ben, who wanted Minda's attention diverted back to himself, leaned over and placed a chubby hand on her cheek. Gently, he turned her head to face him and held a plastic milk truck in front of her nose. "What's this?"

"M-m-milk truck," she stammered.

"Good job," Ben told her solemnly. "Good truck."

A slow, understanding smile spread across her features.

"Ben, come down here." Mrs. Leighton's voice floated up the stairs.

Ben scrambled to his feet at the sound of his mother's call. He was halfway to the door when he remembered the truck in his hand. He turned back into the room and carefully placed it in Minda's palm. "Good truck."

When he had left, Lexi murmured, "Come on. My room's down the hall."

"Nice," Minda commented politely as they entered the bedroom, a room simply but beautifully decorated in soft yellow—Lexi's favorite color.

"Thanks, but I've seen yours. This must look like a matchbox after living in your room."

"It's smaller," Minda acquiesced, "but this is . . . nice."

Lexi sprawled across the bed, crossed her arms, and waited expectantly. Finally, Minda spoke.

"I suppose you're wondering why I'm here."

"Yup."

"I mean, it's not as if we've been getting along or anything."

"Nope."

"So I just needed to make sure that you wouldn't . . . I mean, I had to tell you that you couldn't . . . Not that I expected that you would . . ."

"I don't know what you're talking about, Minda," Lexi chided softly.

Minda gave her a sharp glance. "About my ulcer and my mom and all. You know."

"What about it?"

"I don't want you mentioning it to anyone."

"You mean no one knows you have an ulcer? What if you got sick at school or—"

"It's nobody's business but mine," Minda interjected. "And neither is that business with my mother. She just hasn't been . . . feeling well lately."

"But why did you come here?"

"I don't want you mentioning any of that to anyone. My mom's okay. She's just been having a lot of . . . problems lately." Minda's chin came up proudly. "And I don't want you blabbing any of what you saw."

"I don't 'blab,' Minda. If you knew me better, you'd already know that."

Minda stared at Lexi for a long moment, then slowly, silently sank into a chair near the door. "I didn't really figure you did, but I had to make sure."

"Minda," Lexi began, not quite sure how to say what was whirling about in her mind, "maybe it would *help* to talk to someone about—"

"No way!" Minda's face convulsed with emotion. "And have people repeating what I tell them? Feeling sorry for me because my mom filed for a divorce—"

Minda and Lexi realized at the same moment what Minda had let slip. Minda's eyes narrowed. "You didn't hear me say that. You didn't. It's not true. If you tell anyone, I'll deny it all. I'll say they're separated, but I—"

"Why do you think I'd tell anyone?" Lexi murmured softly. "It's your family's private business. I don't have any right to repeat that."

Minda stared at her so long that Lexi began to wonder if something awful was crawling across her face. Still, she remained silent.

"Do you really mean that?"

"Yes."

It was as though a dam had burst. Minda's face convulsed, releasing a torrent of tears down her cheeks.

"She says she can't live with him any longer and I shouldn't want to either." Minda's words came so fast that they spilled over themselves like a tumble of rocks avalanching down a hillside. "They fight all the time now and Dad leaves and my mother throws things at the door and then she cries 'cause he's gone. Sometimes I hate them both. How can they do this to me?" She took a huge gulp of air. "What am I going to do?"

It was a question Lexi couldn't answer at the moment. She stood up and took Minda's hand in her own and led her to the edge of the bed. Minda sank onto the corner and drew a tearful breath.

"If they split up, my dad says he wants me to come to live with him."

"And your mom?"

"She says there's no way on earth she'd let him 'get' me. She says that I'll stay with her."

"What do you want?"

Minda took a shuddering breath. "I want them together. I want to be a family—like we used to be."

Lexi twisted a stray lock of hair as she assessed the situation thoughtfully. Her friend Cory's parents were divorced. She remembered how Cory had hated the weekends she'd had to pack her bags and leave town to visit her father. It wasn't that she didn't want to see him, Lexi recalled, but that she'd had to leave her home and her friends to do it.

There hadn't been any words that would comfort Cory, and she couldn't think of any now that would help Minda. Just being here with her would have to be enough.

The two girls sat silently for a long time. Ben and

Mrs. Leighton were in the backyard playing with a frisbee. The black lab across the street was barking at something, a squirrel, probably. An occasional car drove by. The noisy hubbub surrounded them like a cocoon.

Minda shifted on the bed and began to speak.

"I guess I thought this would never happen to our family. I thought that my dad's money would help us with any problem we ever had. Boy, was I wrong." She stared out the window at the treetops. "I don't understand, Lexi. Why me? Why is this happening to my parents? They're nice people." She paused, then went on. "At least they *used* to be."

She stared at Lexi as if expecting an answer. Lexi licked her dry lips with the tip of her tongue before she spoke. "Sometimes there aren't any good answers, Minda. Sometimes there aren't any good reasons for things. When Ben was born, my family—"

The sound of the front door opening and closing destroyed the moment. Minda tensed.

"Hi! I'm home!" Mr. Leighton yelled from the bottom of the stairs. "Anyone here?"

"Mom and Ben are out back," Lexi shouted down to him, but the mood between the two girls had been marred. Minda stood up, took a swipe at the running mascara beneath her lashes and moved toward the door.

"I'd better go."

"You don't have to. He'll go outside and—"

"That's okay. I've got things to do anyway." Some of the old Minda returned. "Just remember what I said about our conversations, that's all."

Lexi couldn't help smiling. "Mum is the word."

"It had better be."

"Or what happens?"

Minda gave her a grudging but admiring smile. "You're tough, Lexi. You don't let people push you around, do you?"

"Not if I can help it," she retorted with a grin.

"I'd better get moving." Minda moved reluctantly toward the door.

"Minda . . ."

"Yeah?"

"You can come again."

Minda dipped her head in acknowledgment.

Lexi stood in the doorway until Minda's back had disappeared down the street. When she finally shut the door, Lexi leaned her forehead against the cool wooden panel and closed her eyes.

"Help her, God," she prayed, "and help me to help her, too." How she was going to do that, she couldn't imagine. All she could do now was wait and find out what He had in store for both of them.

Why was it, Lexi wondered, that even though she believed in God and turned to Him in prayer, things seemed so . . . *muddled* sometimes? First Minda, now Todd.

It was only minutes after Minda's strange visit that Todd appeared on the Leightons' front step, his face long and his expression grim.

"Hi, Todd," Lexi said as she opened the door.

Without a word he turned and flopped down on the ground in the front yard and stared up at the cloudless blue sky.

"Want some lemonade? Brownies? One of Ben's ice cream bars?"

He smiled but didn't turn his head. "Feeding me won't make this go away, Lexi, but thanks."

"This" was the sticky situation between Todd and his brother Mike. Though Todd was hesitant to mention it, Lexi knew that there had been real tension between them the past few days. None of the missing tools had turned up at the shop and Todd's name had been noticeably absent from the work roster—except for the hours when Mike was available to work with him.

"You know what the worst part is?" Todd finally ventured, his eyes never leaving the blue expanse of sky. "Having Mike think that I need to be supervised. He makes me count my tools every time I finish a job and keep a checklist so that what I take out, I put back."

"Has anything been missing since then?" Lexi asked.

"No." The word was abrupt and unhappy. "That's what bugs me. It's just showing Mike that I was careless before." Todd rolled to his stomach and faced Lexi. "And I'm *not* careless. I didn't lose those tools. I've thought about it until I feel like my skull will pop. I'm sure I didn't leave any tools on or underneath a hood."

"But then why—"

Todd's eyes glimmered angrily. "Good question, Lexi. That's the one I've been asking myself for days. *Why?*"

Chapter Eight

"It's time, Marilyn. You've got to come to grips with that sooner or later."

"Not yet, Jim. I don't want to talk about it right now." Mrs. Leighton's voice was sharp with anxiety.

"We can't put it off any longer. A decision has to be made. If we're going to do it, we'll have to take care of it this week."

"No! Not yet!"

Lexi grimaced and riveted her eyes on the bowl of cereal she was eating. Her parents were at it again. Disagreements within the Leighton household had been few and far between until recently. Now, every day seemed to bring a new round of tension and heated discussion.

It had all begun with an information packet her father had brought home about a private school for the handicapped that was opening near Cedar River.

"Ben will love it!" her father had enthused. "It will be perfect for him. I've met some of the instructors and—"

"He's too young," Mrs. Leighton had replied

shortly. "I don't want him spending that much time on a bus traveling to and from school."

"It's not like a city bus, Marilyn. The school will send out a van. He'll be supervised from the moment he steps on the bus until you meet him at night. Just think of the opportunities he could have if—"

"He's too young. That's all there is to it." That's when Lexi's mother had whirled out of the kitchen. Soon Lexi and her father had heard the bedroom door slam behind her.

"Your mom can't handle the thought of sending Ben to school that many hours a day," Mr. Leighton had explained to Lexi, "but it's the best thing for him."

"Couldn't he go to the program at the school in this neighborhood?" she'd asked.

"Sure, but this private school can offer him even more. Ben needs every chance, Lexi. Your mom knows that too." Her father had smiled through his worried expression. "She didn't want to send you to kindergarten either. She would have kept you home until you were ten if she'd had her way."

Lexi nodded. Her father was probably right. The private academy *would* be wonderful for her brother, *but*, convincing her mother of that wasn't going to be easy.

Not easy? This decision was going to tear their household apart. Lexi had heard her parents' voices raised long after she'd gone to bed last night.

This morning as Lexi entered the kitchen, she noticed the dark circles beneath her mother's eyes.

"Mom?"

"Hi, Lexi. Want some breakfast?"

"Just juice." She opened the refrigerator and helped herself. "Are you okay?"

"I'll be all right. I just didn't sleep very well."

"It's about this school for Ben, isn't it?"

At the mention of the school, tears welled up in Mrs. Leighton's eyes. "Your father and I just can't agree on this. I don't see why he insists on sending Ben to the academy this year. He'd have to ride in that van for nearly an hour and—"

"Dad says they have lots of special programs there and that Ben would love it—"

"Maybe, if Ben were older . . ." Mrs. Leighton began. Then she set her coffee cup down with a sharp crack. "Your father just doesn't know how a mother feels. He's not even trying to understand how *I'm* feeling. I don't know what's gotten into him!"

Lexi quietly finished her juice and then walked to the door. Her parents were at an impasse over the issue. She meandered to the porch and settled herself against the top step, her back braced against the column of the porch.

So this is what it's like to have your parents disagreeing all the time. She didn't like it—not one bit. It was scary to hear the two people she loved so much argue. Ben's future was important, Lexi mused, but so was her parents' marriage—

The thought struck her with the force of a slamming door. This was how Minda felt all the time— nervous, afraid, unsure of her own future, terrified that her life was going to be ripped apart—and utterly helpless to do anything about it.

Lexi stood up and strode purposefully back into the kitchen. "Mom?"

"Yes, honey?"

"You and Dad aren't going to break up over this or anything, are you?"

Mrs. Leighton's jaw dropped in dumbfounded amazement. "Is that what you think, Lexi? Have we been arguing that much?"

Lexi gave an embarrassed shrug. "Well, it hasn't been very nice around here. I know you love each other and it seems pretty weird to me that you'd forget all that."

"Oh, Lexi, we haven't forgotten." Mrs. Leighton stood up and moved to where her daughter was standing. "Your dad and I have gotten wrapped up— *too* wrapped up—in doing what we think is best for your brother. But if we've gone too far and begun to *hurt* the family instead of help it, then . . ." She was silent.

"I know you don't believe in divorce or anything, but I guess I just needed to hear you say that everything is okay."

"Of course you did. And you also deserve an apology." Mrs. Leighton placed her hands on Lexi's shoulders. "I'm sorry that your dad and I have behaved so badly. We shouldn't have been arguing at all. After all, we both want what's best for Ben." She smiled. "Thanks for reminding me of that."

"Sure, Mom," Lexi returned, a lopsided, embarrassed grin crossing her face. "Maybe Todd's mother, Mrs. Winston, could help you out. She works with all the handicapped programs. She'd be able to tell you if Ben should be at that school or not."

A look of dawning realization washed over Mrs. Leighton's face. "I should have thought of that myself—days ago."

Before her mother could say any more, Lexi maneuvered herself toward the door. Suddenly, she was in a hurry. "Gotta go. There's somebody I think I need to see."

The Hannaford house was quiet as Lexi walked up the front steps. The shades were pulled, the drapes drawn tight. An eerie sensation tickled at the back of Lexi's neck. It was as though no family had lived in the house for a long, long time.

Nervously, Lexi reached out and pressed the doorbell. Her idea to come here, to tell Minda that she could understand her more fully now, had seemed so good and so right at home, but now she began to wonder if she hadn't made a dreadful mistake. The bells bonged and clanged inside the house. Lexi shuddered.

She took one step backward and then another. Perhaps it hadn't been a good time to come. Obviously no one was home. She should have called first. Lexi took two more steps away, then down from the stoop, and onto the sidewalk. Of course, if she'd called, there'd be no promise that Minda would welcome her. Maybe she'd been presumptuous to even come. What hint had she had that Minda would even *care* if Lexi was beginning to understand a little bit of what it was like to have her parents arguing all the time? Another step. Two more. Lexi was ready to turn around and run when the front door opened.

"Lexi!"

She spun around at the sound of the voice. "Minda, hi! I just came by to—what's wrong?" She stared at the girl in the doorway.

Minda's eyes were red and swollen. She squinted against the bright morning light and raised her hand to shield them.

"Wrong? What makes you think anything is wrong?" Minda's voice was a hoarse croak.

"Are you sick? You sound terrible." Lexi moved cautiously toward the door. "I could make you some lemonade with honey. That's good for a sore throat."

"Nothing's going to fix what's wrong with me." Minda turned back and disappeared into the dark house, leaving the door open. Hesitantly, Lexi followed.

"Wouldn't it be better to have some lights on in here?" she ventured.

"No."

"Could I open the curtain or—"

"No."

"A lamp maybe?" Lexi persisted, anxious now to get another look at Minda's face.

"Do what you want."

Cautiously, Lexi flicked on a small table lamp near the door.

A gasp escaped Lexi's lips. The room was in chaos. Pictures were shattered, vases broken, and there was a ragged, gaping hole through the front of the television.

"They had another fight," Minda murmured matter-of-factly, as if a scene such as this was an everyday occurrence. "A big one."

"Your parents?" It was more than Lexi could grasp. Suddenly the tiff over Ben's schooling didn't seem so major.

"He'd been drinking," Minda recounted.

Lexi had no doubt that "he" was Minda's father.

"They called each other terrible names and then somebody threw something. That's when it really started." She pulled on the lapel of the bathrobe she was wearing and squared her thin shoulders beneath the robe. Her attempt at dignity was pathetic to Lexi, who stood staring from the middle of the room. "I tried to stop them, but they wouldn't listen. I don't think they even heard me. Then I cut my foot on a piece of glass." Minda stopped talking and lifted her foot to the edge of a chair so that Lexi could see the jagged cut on the instep.

Minda's voice took on a faint, faraway air. It was as though she was telling a story in which she'd had no part. She looked up at Lexi with hollow eyes. "I was going to clean it up, but I didn't know where to start." Vacantly she prodded at a picture frame with her big toe.

Lexi swallowed. This was scary. Scarier than anything she'd ever encountered before.

"Where is your father now, Minda?"

"Gone."

"Do you know where?"

"His office, maybe. He has a couch there. Or he could be at his club. Or a hotel." She shrugged. "I don't know. He has lots of money. He could be anywhere."

"And your mother?"

"I don't know."

"Didn't she stay here?"

"I suppose so. I heard her crying."

"Do you think she's here now?"

"Maybe. In her bedroom. But I don't want to see her." Her voice hardened. "Ever."

Lexi stepped a little closer. "Minda, maybe you should go and talk to your mother—"

"No."

"But I'm sure that she can—"

"She'll never want to speak to me again."

Lexi blinked. "What?"

"She hates me now and I don't blame her."

"Why should she do that?"

Minda shriveled into a chair, drew her knees to her chest and wrapped her arms around her legs. "Because it's my fault."

"*Your* fault?" Lexi echoed, stunned. "Why?"

"They were fighting about me. That's how it all started. Daddy said that I was a spoiled little . . ." Her voice trailed away. "Never mind."

"I'm sure he didn't mean it. He was probably upset about something else."

"That's what mother said."

"See, I told you."

"But he said that she'd ruined me and that he wanted me to live with him so I could learn about what was really important. He must have meant his business, because he doesn't think anything else is that important." She paused to tuck her feet even deeper beneath her. "Anyway, it's my fault. If I'd been better—"

"Then they'd have found something else to argue about! Your parents' problems don't have anything to do with you!"

"But I should have stopped them. If I'd made

them quit arguing when I was younger, then none of this would have happened. I should have—"

"You can't think it was your fault, Minda. You just can't."

Minda turned a cold, appraising stare on Lexi. "Well, I do. I think it's my fault 'cause I should have stopped them. And do you know who else's fault I think it is?"

Lexi didn't like the cold, angry bite in Minda's voice. "No, I don't."

"I think it's God's."

Chapter Nine

"God's fault?"

"I prayed, Lexi. I really did. I've never meant anything so much in my whole life and . . . nothing . . . nothing happened. Things just got worse. You said He'd be there for me and He wasn't. What kind of a God is that?"

"He's not a faucet that you can turn on and off, Minda," Lexi murmured. "He's not like hot and cold running water."

"Don't be a dope, Lexi," Minda chastised, a twinge of her familiar nastiness surfacing. "I just don't think He cares about me. You, maybe, but not about me."

"Because He didn't answer your prayer," Lexi said, snapping her fingers, "just like that."

Minda's veneer of control was obviously close to breaking. Lexi ached for her, silently praying for the words that might help the anger, the pain.

"God isn't cruel, Minda. We just get Him all mixed up with the bad things in life because of what He's *really* there to do."

111

Minda scowled.

"It's like I've said before, what He wants to do is to support us when the bad things do come along. He doesn't promise to cure everything, but He does promise to be there for us when we need Him. He doesn't send the bad times, Minda, I really believe that. He didn't send a handicapped child to our family to punish us any more than He made your parents separate."

Minda's features relaxed and some of the tenseness disappeared from her eyes. She stared at Lexi thoughtfully. "I don't know, Lexi. I just don't know."

Just then a stirring sound came from the end of the hallway.

"My mom!" Minda looked half scared, half relieved.

Lexi jumped to her feet. "I'd better go." She eyed the door and then the girl across from her. "If you need . . . anything . . . you can call me."

Without a backward look, Lexi slipped out the front door and hurried toward home.

"Alexis! Wake up!" Mrs. Leighton shook her daughter, gently at first, then with more vigor.

"What is it, Mom? Is Todd here already?" Lexi tried to put the spinning room into focus.

"No. It's Ben. I can't find him."

Suddenly Lexi was wide awake. "You can't find him?"

"After you decided to take a nap, Ben and I went out to the flowerbeds for a while. He was sleepy, so he lay down on the couch and I went back to finish my weeding. I just came in and he's not there!" Mrs.

Leighton's voice held a note of panic.

"Did you check the kitchen? I'll bet he woke up and went to find something to eat. You know Ben, always hungry."

"He's not in the house or the yard, Lexi. I've already checked. You've got to help me look for him. You know he has no sense of direction. As soon as he's out of sight of the house, he doesn't know how to get back to it."

Lexi nodded. Ben had been lost once before when she was caring for him, and she knew exactly how her mother felt.

But Ben was not so easily found this time. They searched the area in ever-widening circles, returning to the house every few minutes to see if Ben had made his way back. Finally, Mrs. Leighton admitted, "We have to call your father. We need some help. Would any of your friends be able to look for him?"

"Todd and Peggy will. And Jennifer. I'll call."

"Get on the phone, then. And call your dad first. I'll keep looking."

It was nearly dusk by the time Lexi's hastily gathered patrol had searched the neighborhood and returned to the Leighton yard.

"I've called the police." Jim Leighton came onto the porch, hands dug deep into his pockets. "Do any of you have any other ideas where he might have gone?"

Peggy and Jennifer shook their heads slowly. They were both covered with dirt and grime from crawling through hedges and under porches, searching in all the places a small, curious boy might have gone.

Todd leaned against the porch rail deep in thought. "Maybe he tried to get back to Camp Courage."

"What?" Mr. and Mrs Leighton chimed together.

"He loves running on the race track. Maybe he wanted to go back there and try it again."

"It's worth a try. Todd, you and Lexi come with me. Peggy, you and Jennifer stay with Marilyn and talk to the police." Jim Leighton barked his orders, the concern in his voice edging nearer the surface.

Lexi and Todd followed her father to the car. Fear crept over her like the chilliness of the night air.

Camp Courage was quiet.

"They lock the front gates," Todd whispered, affected by the silence of the evening. "If he discovered that, maybe he'd try to crawl over."

"He could fall. His coordination isn't that developed," Mr. Leighton stated, his voice hushed, not willing to break the silence any more than Todd. Perhaps if they were still, they would hear Ben.

Then a car full of teenagers roared by. And a second. For a moment the noises drowned the small voice calling, "Lexi. Daddy."

It was not until the third carload of teenagers careened around the corner that Todd and Lexi saw Ben—silhouetted in the jagged, moving light of the vehicle's headlights.

"Ben!" Lexi screamed. But it was too late. The driver of the car had not seen the small form until he was upon it.

The sound of flesh against metal reverberated in her ears for the rest of the night.

Dramatically, the sky brightened with headlights, flashing globes and porch lights. But Lexi could not tear her eyes from the crumpled body on the street.

"Ben!" Her screams blended with her father's. She felt herself being pulled away. Clawing wildly, she turned on Todd. "Let me go! Let me go!" Tears blinded her so that her frantic kicking was in vain. Finally Todd's smothering grip lessened.

"You've got to let the paramedics and your father be with Ben. Get in the car. We'll go get your mother and take her to the hospital." Todd was the voice of reason in the midst of chaos.

Nodding, her head bobbing like a springed toy, Lexi repeated, "Mother, we've got to get my mother."

The ride to the hospital took moments, yet forever. Lexi sat rigidly between her mother and Todd, her eyes on the road, unconsciously looking for small forms that might dash into the street.

Jennifer and Peggy had stayed at the house, promising to answer the phone. As he'd left, Todd had extracted a promise from them to try to reach his mother. Mr. Leighton met them at the emergency room door.

"How is he, Jim?"

"Unconscious. Broken bones. That's all I know."

The stark white light and the smells of the hospital corridor were making Lexi sick. Dizzily, she reached for Todd's arm.

"Todd?" Everything felt fuzzy and disoriented. "Will he be all right?"

"I don't know. I hope so. Poor little fellow." Todd glanced at Lexi and then grasped her arm. "I think you'd better sit down."

At the sound of footsteps his eyes lit up in relief—Mrs. Winston was hurrying down the hall. The sound of her tapping heels on the tile ricochetted like bullets around the sterile corridor.

"Todd. How is he?" Mrs. Winston was typically direct, to the point and in control.

"We don't know. The Leightons are in the other corridor. Lexi isn't feeling so good."

"No wonder. You stay here. I'll go see if I can find out anything."

Lexi felt better with the Winstons in charge. She could tap Todd's strength for some of her own. Then she heard the footsteps returning.

Renee Winston's face looked grim. "Well, they just talked to the doctor."

Lexi felt the room spin about her. Todd's steadying hand kept her securely on the chair. "What did they say?"

Renee's eyes darkened until they were like black ink smudges in her white face. "It isn't good, Lexi. Ben's still unconscious."

The room reeled. The black and white checkerboard patterned tile and stark white ceiling exchanged places. Finally, with Todd's calming voice in her ear, the room righted itself.

"She's shivering, Mom."

"I think you should take her home."

"No! What if Ben—" The words stuck in Lexi's throat.

"You can't see Ben now anyway. I'll check with your parents. If the doctors say you can see him, Todd will bring you back immediately."

"But . . ." Fear made her want to run away, yet she couldn't leave Ben.

Mrs. Winston continued, the logic of her words hard to dispute. "Peggy and Jennifer are at your house. See if they can spend the night. Todd will stay as long as you want him to. The four of you are better off at home. Todd's dad and I will stay with your parents. And if they need you or will let you see your brother, I'll call. I promise."

Lexi nodded. She'd feel less helpless at home. There she could gather a suitcase for Ben. He'd miss his teddy bear and blanket. At the thought, the desperate tears flooded through her again.

"Honey, don't cry."

It was Mrs. Leighton's voice.

"Mom!" With a wail, Lexi flung herself into her mother's arms.

"Go home with Todd. We'll call as soon as we know something. The doctor said it could be hours. The Winstons are here with us."

"Mom?"

"Yes, honey," Mrs. Leighton whispered, her cheek resting against the top of Lexi's head.

"I should have been watching Ben for you."

"That's nonsense, Lexi. You can't blame yourself for that. It's no one's fault."

"But if I'd been awake—"

"But I *was* awake, Lexi. And watching the door. I don't know how he slipped by me." Mrs. Leighton gave her daughter a hug. "We *do* take good care of Ben. You know that and so do I. Don't waste your time on blame or guilt. Use it to pray."

They were silent in the rumbling old car on the

way to the Leightons'. Peggy and Jennifer greeted them at the door.

"How is he?" Jennifer's eyes were wide, her forehead creased under her thick blond bangs. Lexi thought disjointedly that she had never seen Jennifer look so vulnerable—or so caring.

"How are *you*?" Peggy echoed.

They had cleaned the dirt and grass from their clothing and straightened the living room. Now they stood nervously by, their faces creased with concern.

"I'm okay. We don't know anything about Ben yet. He's unconscious."

"Ohhh." They gave a corporate sigh, their shoulders slumping simultaneously.

Jennifer, typically, was the first to recover. "So what do we do now?"

"Can you call your folks and ask if you can stay overnight? Lexi's parents are going to stay at the hospital until they know more about Ben's condition." Todd was in command. Lexi felt comforted just watching him take over. Decisions seemed beyond her for the moment.

"When we called our moms to tell them what happened, they both said that if Lexi needed company we should stay. All we have to do is call back and tell them for sure," Jennifer explained.

"And my mother said that you weren't to worry about meals," Peggy added. "She'll bring rolls over for breakfast and a casserole for whenever anyone gets hungry. You're supposed to call anytime, Lexi, if you need anything."

"Mine said that too. And you can stay with me at night if your folks have to go to the hospital," Jennifer rejoined. Then she slumped into a chair, a disconsolate look on her face. "Gee, it hardly seems like enough."

Lexi brought a trembling hand to her face. Hardly enough? Was it only a short time ago that she'd been a stranger in Cedar River? A lonely, suspicious stranger afraid that these people in this new town and state would not accept her and her brother? How quickly and how tragically she'd been proven wrong!

"Lexi, are you all right?" Todd was at her elbow, steering her to the davenport. Gently, he pulled her down beside him. Brushing stray strands of hair away from her forehead, he stared into her eyes. They were soft, warm, concerned.

"Better than you think," she smiled tremulously. "You don't know how much I appreciate all this. Thank you. All of you."

"What are friends for, anyway?" Jennifer asked gruffly. Lexi thought she saw a trickle of moisture on one cheek before the girl turned away.

Peggy, visibly touched, put a light hand on Jennifer's arm. "Come on. I know where the popcorn maker is." The two disappeared silently into the kitchen.

"Oh, Todd," Lexi sighed, letting the pain and fear she'd been harboring surface. "What am I going to do if—"

"It's wasted energy worrying about 'what ifs.' " Todd's abrupt common sense jolted her back to reality.

"You know," she mused, her mind turning back to her growing-up years with Ben, "I always knew how special Ben was—even as a baby. Mom wouldn't let any of us feel sorry about Ben—or for our family. She always said that how we treated Ben could be a lesson for others who had children like him. I'd never been ashamed of Ben until I moved here. Then . . . for a while . . ." Those days flooded back to her with startling clarity and pain.

Just then, Jennifer and Peggy returned with a mixing bowl piled high with popcorn.

"I've got hot chocolate on the stove," Peggy announced. "I know it's summer, but it seemed like the right thing to make. Comforting."

They all nodded. Comforting was what they all needed.

"Is this enough popcorn?" Jennifer wondered, eyeing the small mountain of kernels.

Todd gave a laugh so loud the tension in the room seemed to shatter. "Enough? You could feed the whole high school with that!"

Jennifer grinned. "I guess I got a little carried away."

"What about high school?" Peggy popped through the kitchen door like a red-haired jack-in-the-box.

"Nothing," Jennifer muttered. "Not a thing."

"Well, you don't have to get grumpy about it!" Peggy huffed.

Jennifer looked shamefaced. "Sorry. The mention of school makes me immediately crabby, that's all."

"Why?" Lexi's forehead furrowed in puzzlement. "I love school."

"Maybe *you* do." Jennifer grimaced. "I even hate the thought of it starting again." The venom in her voice startled Lexi.

"All right, girls, break it up," Todd joked. "You can tough it out later about who likes school and who doesn't. Right now I'm more interested in that popcorn."

"Looks like enough to last all night!" Peggy muttered. Suddenly the room was silent again as she added, "Of course, we may be up all night."

At that, Lexi began pacing the room like a caged animal. With a frantic look in her eye, she asked the three watching her, "Why don't they call with some news? *Why don't they call?*"

As her plaintive question died on the air, the telephone rang.

Chapter Ten

As the phone chimed shrilly for a second time and a third, the small group remained frozen. Then Todd jumped up to answer it.

"Hello, Leightons'." He listened for a moment before saying, "Mom, talk slower. I can't understand you." Todd's forehead was creased with effort. "You're jumbling all the words together."

Something horrible had happened. Lexi was sure of it. The room began to spin again. She was about to faint.

Only Todd's voice pulled her back from the abyss into which she was about to tumble. "He's come around, Lexi. Your mom wants you to come to the hospital to see if he recognizes you!" His words were triumphant.

Lexi gripped the arm cushion of the couch, unable to comprehend the good news. "What?"

"He's awake! You're supposed to come right away!" With each word Todd's smile widened. "What are we waiting for?"

"Nothing. Nothing!" She jumped to her feet and

took a flying dive toward Todd. Wrapping her arms around his neck, Lexi threw back her head and laughed. "Let's go!"

Peggy and Jennifer waved them away from the front steps of the Leighton home. Lexi leaned impatiently forward. "Can't you go any faster?"

"Not legally. And we've seen enough of what speeding can do tonight."

Her features clouded. "I wonder who was driving that car. Did you see? All I remember from that minute on is Ben."

Todd's jaw tightened. "Maybe we'd better not talk about that right now, Lexi. Whoever it was must be paying a pretty high price for his carelessness."

"Then you did see who it was!" Lexi twisted to face him. "The police came and took them away, didn't they?"

Todd nodded.

"Was it anyone we know?" Lexi persisted. "Todd, *was* it?"

A long, heavy silence hung between them. Todd seemed to be weighing something in his mind. Finally, he spoke. "I suppose you'll hear who was driving soon enough, Lexi. It was Jerry Randall."

Jerry!

"Are you sure?"

"I saw him go with the policeman. I'm sorry, Lexi."

The memory of Jerry's disgusted face the first time he'd seen Ben was like a jagged knife ripping at her.

"He looked pretty scared. He was crying." Todd's voice was soft. "Can't say that I blame him."

Tough Jerry Randall crying. It was difficult to imagine.

Her parents were waiting for them at the hospital.

Mr. Leighton smiled wanly at Todd. "Thank you for bringing her back. You and your parents have been wonderful."

"Where are Mom and Dad now?"

"They went out for coffee and rolls. The cafeteria is closed for the night. Now that Ben has regained consciousness, Marilyn and I found our appetites returning."

"I want to see him," Lexi insisted. "I have to."

"I'll tell the doctor you're here. Ben's still woozy, but they want to see if he recognizes people he knows." Jim headed toward a distant room.

"Don't be surprised to see Ben all bandaged, Lexi. His arm and several ribs are broken. He's got a deep gash in his head as well."

"Are his legs okay?" Todd asked.

"Yes, why?" Mrs. Leighton turned to him in surprise.

"Then it's possible he can still walk on his own to get his trophies at the Camp Courage banquet."

For the first time in hours, Lexi and her mother laughed.

A white-clad doctor came walking toward the little group. "Where's Lexi? Let's see if your brother recognizes you."

She made two steps down the hall before stopping. "Ben knows Todd too. Maybe he'd recognize him."

The physician nodded briskly. "Very well, then.

You can stay with him only a few minutes."

Ben looked like a toy in the big bed. His hair was tousled across the pillow and his cheeks were as pale as the sheets. His eyes were closed and his thick dark lashes fanned over his cheeks.

As they neared the bed, Lexi whispered, "Ben. Benjamin. Open your eyes and see who's here."

Slowly the almond-shaped eyes opened. Though it seemed a chore, Ben struggled to keep them from shutting again. He looked exhausted. The dark eyes traveled from Lexi to Todd and back again. Lexi could sense her parents and the doctor standing behind them.

Ben licked his bottom lip and swallowed. "Lexi? Big fellow?" He squinted against the brightness of the room as his gaze moved toward Todd.

The doctor inquired, "Big fellow?"

Ben lifted his good arm and pointed at Todd. He said clearly and with feeling, "Big fellow." Then the little hand curled on himself and pointing a finger to his chest, he announced, "Little fellow." Then, satisfied with his performance, he allowed his eyes to drift shut.

Lexi didn't realize she was crying until they returned to the corridor.

"Well, you two certainly did the trick," Mr. Leighton announced. "Looks like Ben's going to be all right."

"Did we miss something?" Todd's parents came toting styrofoam cups of coffee and a package of rolls.

"Ben recognized Todd and Lexi. It's a wonderful sign."

"Thank God!"

"I couldn't agree more," Mr. Leighton's voice quivered. "I'll be thanking Him every day for the rest of my life."

"Now we can all go home and have a good night's sleep," Mrs. Winston concluded. "Especially Lexi. She looks like a ghost."

"I think Marilyn and I will spend the night here," Mr. Leighton announced. "Since Lexi has friends at home, we know she'll have company. If Ben wakes up and is frightened, we can comfort him. That is, of course, if Todd will do us one more favor and take Lexi home."

Todd smiled. "I think that can be arranged."

When Todd arrived at the Leightons' house late the next afternoon, he wore an odd, undecipherable expression.

"Todd? What's wrong?" Lexi blurted.

"I should be asking you the questions," he hedged. "How's Ben?"

"Improving already, Mom says. It's really a miracle, Todd. I've never seen one happen before, but I know this is the real thing."

"Good. Poor Ben shouldn't suffer for the mistakes that other people make." His blue eyes turned cloudy as he added, "No one should have to pay for another's mistakes."

"What is it, Todd? You'd better tell me." Lexi motioned toward a chair. "Sit down."

"Bossy again today, aren't you?"

"Just so relieved that I don't have any manners. Now, what's bugging you?"

Todd stuck out his lower lip and blew a wedge of

blond hair out of his eyes. "I think I'm back in my brother's good graces."

"That's wonderful!" Lexi yelped; then after studying Todd's miserable expression, she leaned back in her chair and added, "Isn't it?"

"Yes . . . no . . . I don't know . . ."

"I think you'll have to explain that one," Lexi observed. "I thought you'd be overjoyed to be out of trouble with Mike."

"I would be—if it hadn't happened like it did." Todd wove his fingers together and hung his hands between his widespread knees.

"How did it happen?" Lexi wondered at his attitude of confusion and unhappiness.

"The missing tools turned up."

"Great! I knew they would!" Lexi clapped her hands together. "And Mike had to apologize for being so rough on you!"

"They were in the trunk of Jerry Randall's car."

"Oh."

"The police came by to ask Mike about them because some of them had the name of his shop engraved into them. He'd identified them all before I even got there."

"Jerry stole them?" Lexi marveled. "But why? He has everything he wants."

Todd shrugged. "I think it was just a dirty trick he was playing. Jerry and I have never gotten along very well, and he probably thought it was funny to see me in hot water with my brother." Todd pounded his balled fist against his leg. "I just *knew* that I'd been putting things back where they belonged; but when they'd turn up missing, I couldn't prove it and

I began to doubt my own memory!" Todd's expression hardened. "And Jerry was laughing all the time."

"He and Minda make quite a pair, don't they?" Lexi observed. "They both look like they have it all; and when you get to know them, they're all weak and empty inside."

Todd nodded. "The police asked if Mike wanted to press charges."

"Is he going to?"

"He told them he'd have to think about it." Todd grinned. "You wouldn't know it by the way he treats me, but Mike's quite a crusader—just like Mom. It wouldn't surprise me if he made Jerry come to the shop and work off his punishment. Mike was already muttering something about 'teaching that punk some common sense.'"

Lexi laughed. "I didn't realize Mike was like that."

"He's a pretty quiet guy, but he does love God— and people. It just pops out in different ways than for most of us."

"Well, I'm just glad that Mike understands that you weren't as careless as he thought you were."

"Yeah. He's apologizing all over himself. I think I'll go back to the garage just to listen to it again." He pushed himself out of the chair and gave Lexi a tweak on the cheek.

As Lexi watched him walk away, she gave a theatrical sigh. "What next?"

For the rest of the week, Lexi spent mornings at Camp Courage and afternoons at the hospital. Ben was a restless patient, who wanted to be entertained endlessly. Lexi was more than willing to be his victim.

On the third day, Jerry Randall came to visit.

He looked thinner, paler, even older. He wasn't the same boy that Lexi remembered from her first days in Cedar River.

"Lexi?" He was carrying a package wrapped in gaily colored paper with a big red bow. His hands were trembling.

Lexi was standing in the hall while the nurses were tending to Ben. When she heard Jerry's voice, she turned to stare at him.

"Hello, Jerry."

"I came to see . . . your brother."

"Why?" Lexi knew she was acting heartlessly, but she felt cold inside, chilled to the core.

"I needed to see for myself that he was all right."

"He's never been 'all right' in your mind, Jerry." Lexi had never felt the likes of the anger that surged within her. He'd hurt Todd terribly and he could have killed Ben.

"I was wrong."

Her eyebrow arched in surprise. This wasn't what she'd expected.

"Wrong?"

Jerry shifted his weight uncomfortably from one foot to the other. "After the accident I began to think. I thought about how I would have felt if your brother had been killed. I realized that it didn't matter that he wasn't like the rest of us. It was still a life I would have taken. And I also realized that his life is as important as yours or mine. I didn't know that until

I did something stupid that almost made him lose it."

The cold core within her began to soften and warm.

"How is he, Lexi? How is he really?"

"He's going to be fine. We're spoiling him rotten. He already uses his cast to slug me to get my attention." She managed a smile at the end of her words.

"When will he be out of the hospital?"

"A couple more days."

"Could you give him this?" Jerry held out the bright package. The bow quivered as he extended his hand.

"No."

"No?" Jerry stepped back, startled.

"I think you should give it to him yourself. Come on, I'll introduce you." Lexi started for the hospital room door as the nurses bustled out ahead of her.

"Can't you just give it to him for me? It's just a teddy bear. I didn't know what else to buy."

"Ben loves stuffed bears. You should give it to him yourself."

Hesitantly Jerry followed her into the room. Ben was sitting up in the bed. He had a puzzle before him on the bedside table. Patiently he was trying to fit Donald Duck's hat into the space above Donald Duck's head. He barely glanced up until the wooden piece was settled into place. Then he gazed at Jerry with intense, studying eyes.

"Ben, Jerry brought you a present."

"Present," Ben smiled widely and held out his good arm.

Nervously, Jerry set the box on the bed near Ben.

Ben tore at the bow like a child opening his last present on Christmas morning. Lifting the lid off the box, Ben peered inside. Lexi could hear a delighted chuckle coming from the inside of the box.

"Bear." Ben pulled out the toy with a flourish.

Jerry had spared no time or expense choosing this toy. The soft brown creature wore a red and white vest with "Benjamin Bear" embroidered across the chest. A pink tongue licked gleefully from one side of the creature's mouth, and wide, soft eyes stared back at Ben.

"What do you say to Jerry, Ben?" Lexi prodded.

"Thank you." Ben had the bear in a stranglehold. He lay back against the pillows with a blissful smile on his face. Nuzzling his nose into the soft fur, Ben closed his eyes and went to sleep. Curled there on the large bed with the bear tucked beneath him, Ben was as beautiful as Lexi could ever remember.

"Come on," she whispered. It took a tug on Jerry's arm to draw him back into the hallway.

"That was very nice of you, Jerry."

"Is he always like that?"

"Like what?"

"Like that—you know, so . . ." Jerry cleared his throat in embarrassment and finished, "Sweet."

"Yes. Ben's always sweet. Sometimes he's naughty and sometimes he's stubborn, but he's always . . . sweet."

"I really had it all wrong, didn't I?" Jerry looked at the hospital room door in wonder. "I thought there was nothing important up there—you know, in Ben's head. But he's a great little guy!"

With that, the coldness encircling Lexi's heart

melted completely. "I'm glad you finally figured that out."

Jerry hung his head. "Guess I'd better go. I'm glad your brother's all right, Lexi. I really am."

"Jerry." She called his name, trapping him. When the boy turned around, Lexi asked, "What happens to you now?"

The boy blanched to the color of milk. Lexi could read apprehension in his dark eyes. "I don't know." Jerry looked as though he wanted to cry. "I've done a lot of stupid things, Lexi." She knew immediately that he was referring to the tools in Mike's shop. "But this thing with your brother was by far the most stupid."

Jerry's shoulders hunched into a defeated slump. With his cockiness gone, he appeared withered and sad. "I never dreamed all this could happen, Lexi. We were racing—just for the fun of it. I never thought . . ." He laughed bitterly. "*That's* my problem. I never thought—about a lot of things."

"What will they do to you?"

"I could go to jail."

"Jail? But you go to school!"

"If the judge decides the offense was serious enough, I could serve the sentence weekends—for as long as he decides."

"And if he decides to do something else?"

"My attorney says because of my age and no previous record, I could get by with community service. The judge would pick the place and tell me how many hours I'd have to spend." Jerry's voice cracked. "I'd gladly do anything to stay out of jail, Lexi. But I'd want to go to jail if I'd killed your brother. I'd deserve it." Silently he turned and walked down the hall.

She sighed and sank into the chair next to Ben's door, weary from the emotional roller-coaster she'd been riding. She wished she, too, could curl up and take a nap. Lexi closed her eyes and leaned her head against the wall.

It was Minda's urgent whisper that woke her.

"Lexi? Are you asleep?" Minda was pressing her face close, and when Lexi's eyes flew open, Minda jumped. "You startled me!" she accused, Minda-like.

"*I* startled you? But you woke *me* up!"

"Hospitals give me the creeps," Minda said and gave an exaggerated shudder for emphasis.

Lexi fought the urge to smile. "Then what are you doing here?"

An odd look passed over Minda's features. "I don't know, really. I don't want to be here." She glanced disdainfully around. "Creepy place."

That erased any thoughts Lexi might have had that she was finally beginning to understand Minda.

"I just figured since you were there for me, I'd . . ." Minda's voice trailed away in embarrassment.

A warm rush of surprise and gratitude filled Lexi. Maybe there was hope for Minda, after all.

"That's very nice of you. Thanks."

"Yeah, sure." Minda eyed the hall restlessly. "Kind of makes us even, doesn't it? Like we don't owe each other anything anymore."

"You could say that," Lexi agreed, her hopes for Minda's change of heart dashed. *Even?* Is that the best she and Minda could be? *Even?*

Minda dropped onto the seat next to Lexi's. "So how is he? The kid, I mean?" she demanded.

"He's going to be okay."

"Good. He's not such a bad little guy." Minda dug into her pocket and took out a toy truck. "Give him this, will you? Tell him it's a 'good truck.'"

Her look was so vulnerable, so wistful, that Lexi dared to voice the question that had been haunting her. "How are things at home?"

Minda's face hardened. "About the same, I guess. My parents are going to counseling. I have to go, too. They aren't getting the divorce until they see if this helps." Minda kicked angrily at the leg of a chair. "Why is everything so hard? Why can't someone— anyone—just make them work it out?"

Her jaw tensed and she stared intently at the tile floor. When she spoke again, her voice was harsh and resentful. "The counselor says these things take time. You say God takes His time. Who's in a hurry for things to be better but me? No one!"

Sensing that she was treading on thin ice, Lexi asked, "What are you going to do in the meantime?"

"Live with Mom and visit Dad at his apartment, I guess." Minda's expression was etched with pain. It's just all mixed up, Lexi."

"Have you thought about—" Lexi began.

Minda gave her a withering stare. "I know, I know. God. Right?"

Lexi nodded. "He's—"

"I'm just not sure I'm ready for that, Lexi. I'm not sure I could believe like you do." She gave a wry, humorless laugh. "God's never been a big topic of conversation at our house."

Impulsively, Lexi leaned forward. "I can't make you believe anything Minda. All I can tell you is that

He *is* here for you. Even if you don't realize it yet."

Minda stared at Lexi for a long moment. "Maybe. Maybe not. I'll think about it."

Then, in a lightning change of mood, Minda began to fidget in her chair.

"You don't have to stay if it makes you uncomfortable," Lexi told her.

"You don't mind?" Minda asked, obviously eager to be away—far away.

"No. Not now that I know Ben's going to be all right."

"Maybe I'll go then." She backed away, one hand raised in a final salute. "See ya."

"See ya." A smile crept across Lexi's face.

That's how Todd and Mrs. Leighton found her some moments later.

"My goodness, you look thoughtful and mysterious!" Marilyn teased, brushing a long blond lock of hair across Lexi's shoulder.

"It's been that kind of morning."

"Why don't you go with Todd. He said he'd take you out for something to eat. I'll stay with Ben. I'll be glad when he gets home. Then we can quit spoiling him so unmercifully."

"Okay. Anything you want me to do?" Lexi uncurled from the hard seat. She brushed her hands across the legs of her pale pink jumpsuit and stood.

"Go and have some fun. You haven't done enough of that lately. Just be home for supper. Hear that, Todd?"

Todd, looking particularly handsome in a bright teal shirt, saluted playfully. "Yes, ma'am." It wasn't until they were seated in the little coupe that he spoke again. "Want to talk about it?"

Lexi stretched wearily against the seat. "How do you know there's something to talk about?"

"I can read you like a book, Lexi Leighton. What happened?"

"Jerry Randall came to the hospital today."

Todd whistled through his teeth.

"And after he left, Minda came."

"No wonder you look like you've been through the wringer! What did they want?"

"Jerry apologized." Lexi leaned her head against the seat and closed her eyes.

"About the accident?"

"And about the way he thought and acted about Ben." Lexi shifted in her seat so she could look straight at Todd. "What's going to happen to him?"

Todd lifted his shoulders in a wondering gesture. "He's in deep trouble, that's all I know." He was silent a moment before adding, "He told Mike and the police pretty much what I'd guessed—that he wanted to see me in some kind of trouble and he'd thought the tool thing was just a prank." Todd snorted. "Some prank."

"That's all he said?"

"No. There was more. Weird too. Do you know why he said he did it?"

"No."

"Because he was *jealous*!"

"Of you?"

"Sure, of me. But it just doesn't figure. Why would he be jealous of me? I'm working my tail off for every dime I earn, and he gets a weekly allowance for doing nothing."

"Who gives it to him?"

"I don't know. His uncle, I suppose."

"His uncle?"

"Yeah. That's who Jerry lives with. His mom and dad are oil rig engineers in the Persian gulf or something weird like that. They dumped Jerry off in Cedar River when he was about eight. He's been living with his aunt and uncle ever since."

"Do they come to see him?"

"Once in a while. I think they were here last year for a couple of days. He talks about it for weeks and flashes around all the stuff they've brought him. Jerry has every electronic gadget known to mankind. He's really a pain in the neck after his parents have come."

"What about his aunt and uncle?"

Todd looked at her strangely. "What about them?"

"Is Jerry close to them?"

"Who knows? They don't come to school plays or anything. They pretty much let Jerry do what he wants."

"And you wonder why he's jealous of you?" Lexi murmured.

"Yeah."

"You just gave some pretty great reasons."

"Like what?"

"Like having parents who don't want him living with them. Like staying with relatives who don't even come to see him in a class play. Like having to pretend it's great to have rich parents who travel when all he wants is plain, ordinary parents who stay home to help him grow up!"

A sheepish expression spread across Todd's face. "I never thought about it that way before."

Lexi smiled. "I guess Minda and Jerry are a lot alike, huh? Parent troubles. Bad ones."

"How was Minda today?"

Lexi sighed. "I'm not so sure about her."

"Well, that's nothing new with Minda."

"But there's something . . ." She couldn't quite explain it, Lexi decided. It was as if she'd seen a tiny flicker of light at the end of a dark passage and it had disappeared as quickly as it had come. Maybe, just maybe, God had pried open a little spot in Minda's heart.

"Sounds like you and Ben have made some progress."

"Progress? What do you mean by that?" She straightened up to stare at Todd.

"Did you ever think either Jerry or Minda would be visiting you and Ben?"

"No, I guess not." A smile tipped up the corner of her lip.

"Or that you'd even *understand* them?"

"I didn't figure that would *ever* happen!"

"Point made." Todd grinned. "You're going to have to learn it sooner or later, Lexi Leighton. You just never know what's going to happen next in Cedar River!"

What price will Jerry have to pay for his recklessness? And why does Jennifer hate school so intensely? Find out in Cedar River Daydreams, 3, *Jennifer's Secret.*

A Note From Judy

I'm glad you're reading *Cedar River Daydreams*! I hope I've given you something to think about as well as a story to entertain you. If you feel you have any of the problems that Lexi and her friends experience, I encourage you to talk with your parents, a pastor, or a trusted adult friend. There are many people who care about you!

Also, I enjoy hearing from my readers, so if you'd like to write, my address is:

Judy Baer
Bethany House Publishers
6820 Auto Club Road
Minneapolis, MN 55438

Please include an addressed, stamped envelope if you would like an answer. Thanks.